Chinese Fairy Tale Feasts

A Literary Cookbook

First published in 2015 by
CROCODILE BOOKS
An imprint of Interlink Publishing Group, Inc.
46 Crosby Street, Northampton, Massachusetts 01060
www.interlinkbooks.com

Simultaneously published in Canada and the UK by Tradewind Books

CATALOGING-IN-PUBLICATION DATA AVAILABLE FROM THE LIBRARY OF CONGRESS
ISBN 978-1-56656-993-4

Book design by Jacqueline Wang

The type is set in Archer and Sofia Pro.

10 9 8 7 6 5 4 3 2 1

Printed and bound in Korea

Chinese Fairy Tale Feasts

A Literary Cookbook

Tales by
Paul Yee

Illustrations by
Shaoli Wang

Recipes by
Judy Chan

Foreword by
Jane Yolen

Crocodile Books, USA

An imprint of Interlink Publishing Group, Inc.

www.interlinkbooks.com

Contents

For Jill and Ronald Holla, who cross cultures and languages.—PY

To my mother, Xiyun Li.—SW

For my mother and sister, who are great passionate cooks.—JC

Foreword: A Note to the Readers of this Book

When my daughter, Heidi Stemple, and I began writing *Fairy Tale Feasts* ten years ago, we hadn't thought beyond that one book. I retold the fairy tales, and she made the recipes. It was a partnership that worked well.

Then we wrote a second book, *Jewish Fairy Tale Feasts*, drawing upon our own cultural background.

I am delighted to see the series continue—this time with a book written by the award-winning writer Paul Yee. He has amassed an important body of work, my favorite being *Tales from Gold Mountain: Stories of the Chinese in the New World,* which showcases the terrific storytelling ability now seen in *Chinese Fairy Tale Feasts*.

Yee draws on his deep knowledge of Chinese culture and history to create and retell these tales. Being a storyteller, he has heard them, read them, spoken them, and here shares them once more—they seem to be in his bones. They are full of witches, monkey gods and magic makers. The tales speak of monks, peasants, greedy leaders and honest beggars. They unearth the full variety of human nature and experience.

What they all have in common is food. Why food? Because food is an all-powerful motivator. Without it, we cannot live; with it we are productive, we have power, we thrive.

What distinguishes us from other animals is not that we use tools or have opposable thumbs, but our ability to make stuff up, tell stories. And the connection between food and stories is profound and clear. Both are infinitely changeable, suiting the needs of the maker and the consumer.

Storytellers never tell a story the same way twice—but pay attention to the audience. They ask: what is the season, the time of day, the age of the listener and notice if the audience is restless or paying rapt attention. They not only tell a tale, they reshape it, mouth to ear.

Cooks do the same—changing recipes according to the season, the time of day, the age of the eaters. Cooks change the food according to what's in the cupboard or the refrigerator, and the eaters' allergies or tastes. Or change the dish to better reflect the culture within which they are cooking. Tongue to tummy.

And the bright, personable illustrations in the book by Shaoli Wang add the spice to both meals—story and food.

If you want to tell the stories that Paul Yee offers up here or want to make Judy Chan's marvelous recipes, you can, with the help of this book. But even more fun: learn the tales, learn how to make each dish, and then change both, bit by bit by bit—adding, subtracting, rearranging. Judy Chan's food recipes, like Paul Yee's stories, will go down better as you change them and make them your own. Surprisingly, they'll become yours the more you pass them on.

Yum.

Jane Yolen

A Note from the Cook

I was fortunate to have a mother who loved to cook delicious dishes—both Chinese and Western style. I marveled at how she could put together multiple courses for a Chinese meal on a daily basis without any recipes or training. She seemed to do it by a special natural instinct. She encouraged both my sister and me to join her baking and cooking escapades in the kitchen. We now explore many different cuisines; however, at the heart of our cooking passion is the Chinese food that we grew up with.

I now share my passion for great Chinese dishes with my students. Some of the recipes in this book have been used in my classroom, and I developed others from memories of what my mother or other relatives used to cook. Most of these recipes represent traditional Chinese food, and a few were modified to suit current tastes. Paul Yee's stories have been inspirational and have reintroduced me to some traditional Chinese folk tales.

When you try these recipes, please feel free to adjust them to suit your tastes and the availability of ingredients. Most of the ingredients in these recipes can be found in supermarkets. If you have an Asian supermarket or a Chinatown nearby, explore them and discover new culinary delights.

May I remind you that young aspiring cooks need adult supervision in the kitchen, especially when using knives and cooking at the stove. When cooking Chinese food, a significant amount of time needs to be devoted to the preparation of the ingredients. Many recipes involve tasks suitable for a beginner cook, while others are more appropriate for an experienced one. In this way, they provide the opportunity for different generations to work together. So settle into a story, tie your hair back if it is long, put on an apron, wash your hands, and enjoy this unique culinary and literary experience!

Judy Chan

Banquet of Waste

宴會大浪費

One of the Eight Immortals was named Iron Crutch. In the days before Iron Crutch joined the gods, he had been a powerful sorcerer. He had the power to let his soul leave his body and fly through the air, traveling great distances.

During one such journey, one of the sorcerer's students came across him, lying still and cold. "Ai-yah, my master is dead!" the student wailed. In great sorrow, he burned the body.

Iron Crutch's soul returned to find only ashes where his body had lain, so he searched far and wide for a person who had recently died. At last he found one—an old lame beggar with blackened skin, dressed in smelly rags and surrounded by flies. In this guise, Iron Crutch became the patron god of poor people all over China.

One day at the beginning of spring, Iron Crutch was begging for food at the back door of a foul-tempered merchant's house. The merchant, Boss Kuang, had grown rich by setting high prices and paying low wages. When one of the office clerks injured his back, Boss Kuang fired him; after his chief cook scorched a chicken, Boss Kuang fined him 100 taels; after his wagon driver splashed mud on Boss Kuang's coat, he made him pay for a new one.

The merchant's daughter, Mo-jun, however, was very different from her father. She saved leftovers to feed the beggars who gathered at the back door, and on the back porch she kept a pot of drinking water and blankets for the homeless. When Iron Crutch knocked at the door, Mo-jun filled his begging bowl with boiled rice, vegetables and meat.

At the end of summer, when Boss Kuang turned sixty, he held a grand banquet. To prepare for the big day, his servants repaired the road in front of his mansion. They filled the potholes with uncooked rice and covered them with a wool carpet.

The servants also spread a thick layer of rice on the ground by the front door, and laid another carpet on top. The grain made a soft and crunchy path for his guests.

Mo-jun saw this and begged her father to stop wasting food, but he refused. She ran out to scoop up the rice, but Boss Kuang grabbed her and locked her in her room.

Mo-jun wept into her pillow.

The guests arrived in horse-drawn carriages and sedan chairs, wearing long-sleeved gowns embroidered with threads of gold and silver.

Beggars gathered to watch the procession.

Iron Crutch limped up, surrounded by flies, just as the guests were being ushered in. He called out to the servants, "Your master is hosting a grand banquet. Can you spare a small dish for me?"

Boss Kuang shouted, "Go away, you wretch, and take your flies with you! Go, before I come and beat you."

"May I take a few grains of rice from under the carpets?"

"Touch one grain of rice and you will be jailed for stealing!"

Iron Crutch promptly bent over and took a few grains of rice.

A guard immediately seized him, and Boss Kuang sent for the judge.

Bowing before the judge, Boss Kuang said, "Your Honor, this beggar stole my rice."

"No, Your Honor, I did not steal. When Boss Kuang's servants dumped the rice onto the ground, he was throwing it away. It didn't belong to him anymore. Surely that is the law of the land."

Boss Kuang bowed again. "Your Honor, I covered the rice with my carpet. I am like a roadside seller of rice porridge. As long as his pot is covered, the porridge is his, and everyone must pay for it."

The judge frowned. "Boss Kuang is right. I cannot help you. Please accept my regrets."

Boss Kuang smirked. "See, I was right all along."

Boss Kuang needs a lesson, Iron Crutch thought. *But I must not punish him too harshly, for his daughter is generous.*

Bong! Bong! Bong! Men beating great gongs announced the start of the meal. Delicious aromas drifted from the kitchen and onto the street. Imagining the banquet guests sitting down in front of sumptuous dishes, the beggars moaned and wailed.

Suddenly the front door flew open, and the guests came running out. Some tripped on their long sleeves and fell on their faces. "Ow!" they cried.

One guest told his horseman, "When the dishes were brought to the tables and uncovered, clouds of flies flew out."

Another person said, "Servants tried to drive them off, but couldn't."

"We couldn't even eat!" a woman exclaimed. "If we opened our mouths, flies rushed in."

"The swarms of flies were so thick, they darkened the room."

The guests bolted into their carriages, and stormed off.

Soon Boss Kuang ran out, holding his bamboo pole. His face was as red as an overripe tomato. "You did this!" he screamed, pointing at Iron Crutch. "You sent your filthy flies to wreck my banquet!" Then he hit Iron Crutch hard on the head with his bamboo pole.

Iron Crutch fell, sending his soul from his body. He stopped breathing.

Some of the beggars ran to get the judge.

Boss Kuang's men hurried to hide the body. Two of them grabbed Iron Crutch's hands and feet. They heaved and pulled, but couldn't move him. Two more servants came to help. To their surprise, they found the body as heavy as an elephant. A worried Boss Kuang rolled up his sleeves and joined in. But even five men couldn't lift the fragile bundle of skin and bones.

When the judge arrived, Boss Kuang said, "Your Honor, I caught this filthy beggar stealing my rice again. I struck him gently, but he fell over dead."

The judge searched through Iron Crutch's rags and found a slip of paper. It read:

No matter how rich or generous,
You cannot step on the penniless.
All must eat, no matter where they live.
The daughter knows, and always gives.
Kuang must pay for bringing me down.
Send him to sweep every road in the town.

When Boss Kuang saw this, he sent his men to release his daughter from her room. Mo-jun cried out when she recognized Iron Crutch. "Poor man! Is he dead?" She knelt and touched his forehead. Tears filled her eyes.

Just then Iron Crutch summoned his soul back into his lifeless body. "No, young mistress, I am very much alive. Please, help me stand."

Two of the beggars stooped to lift him up. He was as light as a feather.

Boss Kuang fell to his knees. "I have insulted the gods."

He turned to Mo-jun. "My daughter, I am sorry I have been so blind. I have learned a great lesson." Then he said to the beggars, "Please, come inside and enjoy our feast."

To everyone's amazement, not a single fly was to be seen anywhere.

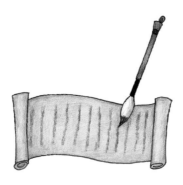

IRON CRUTCH, THE GOD

Iron Crutch, Defender of the Poor, was one of the Eight Immortals from the Taoist tradition. Each of these popular gods had once been a human being—male, female, young, old, rich, poor, noble and humble. As a group, the Eight Immortals represented happiness, long life, prosperity and wisdom. Each god had his own magical tool: a fan, a crutch, a flute, a sword, a clapper, a whisk, a flower basket or a gourd. Each was the patron saint of a profession, such as barber, actor, musician, housewife, herbal healer, soldier, scholar or florist.

People believed that the Immortals had the power to give life and destroy evil. In China's storytelling tradition, stories about Iron Crutch encourage people to be kind to the less fortunate.

RICE

People in China have grown rice as a food crop for over five thousand years. Chinese scientists recently found that during the Ming dynasty (AD 1368–1644), sections of the Great Wall of China were built using a mortar made from sticky rice and slaked lime. This mortar held the bricks together tightly and stopped weeds from growing between them, making the wall more stable and helping it to last. Parts of the Great Wall were built in the fifth century BC.

Congee (Rice Porridge)

鷄 湯 白 粥

Congee or "jook" is a rice porridge that is popular for breakfast or a light meal. Congee is versatile, and can be enhanced by adding various ingredients. My mother always used the turkey bones from Thanksgiving to make a rich stock that she would use to make it.

INGREDIENTS

¾	cup	long grain white rice or ¼ cup short grain and ½ cup long grain
8	cups	chicken broth, homemade from Poached Chicken (page 158) or store bought
1	inch	fresh ginger
1	tsp	salt
¼	tsp	white pepper
2	cups	shredded cooked chicken or julienned ham or Chinese BBQ pork or raw shrimp, deveined & coarsely chopped
4		dried Chinese mushrooms (optional), soaked in hot water, stems removed and thinly sliced

FLAVOR ENHANCERS & GARNISHES

- 3–4 green onions
- soy sauce and sesame oil, to taste
- roasted and salted peanuts (optional), coarsely chopped
- cilantro (optional), coarsely chopped

EQUIPMENT

- measuring cups & spoons
- liquid measuring cup
- sieve
- heavy bottomed pot
- teaspoon
- cutting board
- chef's knife
- wooden spoon
- ladle

METHOD

1. In the sieve, rinse rice under cold water to remove excess starch. Shake out water.

2. In the heavy bottomed pot, bring the rice and chicken broth to a boil.

3. Meanwhile, scrape the skin off the ginger with a teaspoon, cut into 3 pieces and smash against cutting board with the blade of the knife. Add the ginger, salt and white pepper to the rice and broth mixture. When at a full boil, reduce heat to medium low and simmer, stirring occasionally with a wooden spoon. Simmer for about 1 hour or until the rice thickens into a porridge-like consistency.

4. While the congee is cooking, wash the green onions. Cut off the root ends and thinly slice on a diagonal from the white end to half way up the green part. Discard the upper green part to avoid any bitterness. Set aside.

5. If using shrimp, add to congee and simmer until opaque and cooked. If using Chinese mushrooms, simmer in congee until tender. If adding cooked meats, heat until hot.

6. To serve, ladle congee into soup bowls and top with sliced green onions. Season with soy sauce and sesame oil. Sprinkle chopped peanuts and cilantro, if desired.

Stretch and Fold, Stretch and Fold

千拉百叠

One summer many centuries ago, the rains failed to fall in North China. The wheat crop withered in the countryside, and people went hungry. When the farmers found out that the chief's great storeroom was stacked high with sacks of grain, they shouted with joy, "We're saved! Our chief will help us."

So the farmers, with their children and grandchildren, with their parents and grandparents, all hurried to the wall of sturdy logs surrounding the chief's great storeroom.

But the chief was saving the grain to feed his warriors. Looking out from the watchtower, he gasped when he saw the swarm of people below.

"Close the gates!" he bellowed to his guards, and they ran to obey.

Just then the chief's son came running up the watchtower stairs. "Father, people are hungry! Why lock them out?"

"There's not enough food. We can't feed everyone."

"But even little children and babies have come."

"Our warriors must be fed first."

"But . . ."

The chief raised his hand. "Enough. Now go."

His son trudged away, saddened.

Outside the gates, the crying of hungry babies and the wailing of thirsty youngsters filled the air.

So the chief's son ran to his mother. *Maybe she'll tell the servants to open the storehouse and give them grain.* "Ma," he said, "please talk to father. Shouldn't we feed the hungry people?"

"Yes, we should," his mother said, nodding. She turned and hurried away.

Soon she returned, shaking her head. "Your father won't listen to reason."

The boy ran to the kitchen to talk to the servants. "My friends, please take bread and grain to give to the farmers and their families. They're starving."

"Yes, young master!" The servants bowed. Some hurried to the storeroom for sacks of grain, others packed up steamed bread.

But when they reached the gates, the guards were standing fast, pointing their spears at them. "No one is allowed to leave," the guards shouted. "If you disobey, you will be flogged."

So the servants put the grain back and returned to the kitchen with the bread.

"Young master, we failed," one servant said, bowing deeply.

"The guards stopped us," another said, "so we couldn't do anything.

The boy went back to his mother. "Ma, Father ordered the guards to stop anyone from going to the farmers."

"Remember that small hole in the wall?" she asked.

"The place where I played when I was little?"

"That's it," she said. "Go there and wait."

Secretly, the chief's wife went to the kitchen and grabbed a ball of dough, and wrapped it in cloth. Then she went to the storeroom and took a sack of grain. Finally she joined her son at the wall.

"Hurry through the hole, son," she said, handing him the ball of dough. "I'll pass you the grain once you're on the other side."

Just as the boy wriggled through the hole in the wall, the guards rushed up with their spears. His mother tried to shove the sack through, but the guards tore it from her hands.

"You will be punished!" they shouted.

The frightened son ran. All he had was the ball of dough.

Soon he was surrounded by the farmers and their families.

"Have you brought us any grain?" one farmer asked.

"Have you brought us any bread?" said another.

"We're so hungry," cried a third.

Oh no! I don't have enough to feed even one family, the boy thought, staring at the ball of dough in his hands. *What will I do?*

Desperate, he pulled apart the dough, reaching out as far as his arms could go. He folded it over into two layers and stretched it out again. Then he folded the two layers of dough to make four. Again he pulled them out as far as his arms could stretch.

Oh no. There still isn't enough.

So he folded the four layers to make eight. Then he pulled them out again, as far as his arms could stretch.

Oh no. There still isn't enough.

But when he glanced at the hungry faces all around, he persisted. He folded the eight layers of dough to make sixteen, pulled them out, and folded again.

The sixteen became thirty-two. And the thirty-two became sixty-four. The sixty-four became one hundred and twenty-eight. And the one hundred and twenty-eight became two hundred and fifty-six.

His arms grew tired, but he did not stop. Each time he stretched out the dough, the layers became thinner. Soon they turned into long strings, hanging from his hands like vines.

He cut off the strings and handed them to the farmers. Each time he broke off the pieces, he found that he was still holding more. There was always more dough. There was no end to the dough.

"A miracle!" cried the farmers.

"A miracle!" shouted the guards on the nearby towers, and they ran to tell the chief.

"Ai-yah!" the chief exclaimed, shaking with fear. "Heaven is watching over my peasants! Ai-yah, now I am in big trouble!"

He called to his warriors, "Quick, bring sacks of grain. Quick, open the gates!"

The chief, his wife and all their servants handed out sacks of grain and trays of bread to the hungry farmers and their wives, their children, their parents and their grandparents.

Then the chief bowed deeply to his wife and son. "I was so selfish. I am sorry," he said, praising their kindness, "you were correct."

Everyone cheered.

The next year, after the rains fell, the harvest was good. The farmers milled the grain. They mixed flour and water to make balls of dough just like the one the chief's son had carried through the hole in the wall. Then they stretched and folded the dough, over and over, until there were great piles of noodles for every family.

This is a tale about how one of China's most beloved foods came to be.

NOODLES IN CHINA

The world's first noodles were discovered in China along the Yellow River at a site that is four thousand years old. The ancient noodles were preserved in an earthenware pot that had fallen into a river, its mouth sealed by clay. Scientists found those noodles to be like today's la-mian 拉面 *noodles, which are made by folding and stretching dough over and over by hand.*

Today, Chinese noodles are made from wheat or rice flour, or from mung bean starch. They can be as thin as needles 粉絲, *as round as chopsticks* 拉面, *or long and flat like mending tape* 沙河粉. *They can be eaten hot or cold, in soup, plain or spiced.*

The names of some of China's best-known noodle dishes are hot dry noodles 熱乾面, *sao-zi noodles* 臊子面, *dan-dan noodles* 擔擔面, *chow-mein* 炒面 *and noodles with bean sauce* 炸醬面.

There is archeological evidence that people in other parts of the world, such as Italy and the Middle East, also invented their own versions of noodles.

CHINESE PROVERB

養兒防老，積穀防饑

Translation: Raise children to avoid old age;
　　　　　　　　 store grain to avoid famine.

Meaning: Always plan for the future.

Dan-Dan Mian
(Noodles with Peanut Sauce)

擔擔面

This popular spicy Sichuan noodle dish was named after the poles that street vendors used to carry their noodles, sauces and pots. The following version of dan-dan mian captures the essence of this Sichuan noodle dish with its peanut sauce, but adds fresh vegetables. The spiciness can be adjusted to your personal taste. Some chefs stretch and fold the dough into noodles in front of their customers.

INGREDIENTS

1	lb	fresh steamed egg noodles
1		carrot
½		English cucumber
2	tbsp	sesame oil
1		red bell pepper
1		yellow bell pepper
¼	cup	green onions, thinly sliced on the diagonal
¼	cup	cilantro, coarsely chopped
⅓	cup	roasted peanuts, coarsely chopped

PEANUT SAUCE

2		medium-sized garlic cloves, minced
1	inch	fresh ginger, peeled and minced
2	tsp	peanut or vegetable oil
½	cup	natural smooth peanut butter
2	tbsp	sesame oil
2	tbsp	soy sauce
2	tbsp	rice vinegar
1	tbsp	honey or brown sugar
¼	cup	hot water
1	tbsp	hoisin sauce (optional)
¼	tsp	hot chilli garlic sauce (optional)

EQUIPMENT

- measuring cups & spoons
- liquid measuring cup
- medium-sized pot
- colander
- large bowl
- cutting board & knife

- vegetable peeler
- grater
- small pot
- wooden spoon
- tongs
- serving platter

METHOD

1. Bring to a boil a medium-sized pot of water.

2. As the water comes to a boil, wash all the vegetables in cold water. Peel the carrot and cucumber.

3. When the water is at a full boil, add the fresh noodles and cook for 3–5 minutes. Cooked noodles should be tender yet still firm. Drain in the colander immediately. In a large bowl, toss the cooked noodles with the sesame oil to prevent noodles from sticking together. Set aside.

4. Cut the peppers in half and remove seeds. Slice the halves into thin strips (¼-inch wide) and then dice. Grate the carrot and set aside.

5. Cut the cucumber in half lengthwise. Cut each half of the cucumber in half lengthwise again. Then cut crosswise into ¼-inch small wedges. Set aside.

6. To make the sauce, gently heat the peanut or vegetable oil in the small pot, and sauté the minced ginger and garlic until fragrant. Add the remaining sauce ingredients and blend with the wooden spoon. The consistency of the sauce should be similar to thick whipping cream. Add additional hot water or gently simmer to get the right consistency. Taste and adjust seasoning.

7. Add the vegetables to the bowl of noodles, and toss. Drizzle in the peanut sauce. Using the tongs, gently mix the sauce evenly into the noodle-vegetable mixture. Transfer to the serving platter and garnish with the cilantro and roasted peanuts. This dish can be served warm or cold. Enjoy!

A Wondrous Pear Tree

梨樹開花

One day long ago at a busy market, a farmer's wife was standing by her wooden cart, shouting, "Juicy pears for sale! Sweet pears, freshly picked early this morning!"

Eager shoppers surrounded her, handing her money.

An old Taoist monk limped over and held out his hand. "Kind Aunty, please give me a pear. Just a little one." His voice was raspy. His face was thin, his body gaunt. His robe was patched in many places. A gourd of water hung from a cord around his neck.

The farmer's wife avoided looking at him, but the monk

slipped in between the shoppers and came right up to her. "Please, Aunty, please show some heart. I have not eaten in two days."

"My pears are for sale. I need the money to feed my children."

"You have so many beautiful pears," the monk said, pointing to the huge pile on her cart. "I only ask for one."

"No, not even one. Go away."

The monk didn't move. "Please!" he begged. "Just one small pear."

"No!" she shouted. "No! No!"

Everyone crowded around. A noisy argument in public was always fun to watch.

Someone shouted out, "Woman, don't be so stingy!"

"Give the poor monk a pear," another insisted.

A third cried, "He's so hungry!"

Soon a soldier wearing armor clomped over. He was carrying a long spear, and a heavy sword was sheathed at his waist. The soldier reached into a purse hanging from his belt, pulled out a few coins and handed them to the farmer's wife. "Give the monk your juiciest pear."

"Thank you, young man," the monk said, taking the pear and bowing. "You have a good heart."

He turned to the jostling crowd and shouted, "Thank you for speaking up for me, good people." Then he bit into the pear, broke it open and took out the seeds. Kneeling down, he scratched a hole in the ground and dropped in the pear seeds, covering them with soil. He watered them from the gourd around his neck.

Soon a sliver of bright green sprang up.

Everyone gasped and pushed forward.

The green shoot grew into a leafy stalk. In an instant, it turned into a sapling, and by the next instant, it was a sturdy young tree with thick bark. Branches shot out from the trunk, thrusting up into the sky. Fragrant pink blossoms bloomed, and fruit began to take shape.

Soon the tree was heavy with ripened pears, all dark yellow.

"Friends, all this fruit is for you," the monk called out, stepping aside.

Everyone rushed to the tree, bringing ladders and boxes to stand on.

In no time, all the pears were gone.

Shouts rang out.

"Very sweet!"

"The best pears ever!"

"Delicious!"

"Juicy!"

The farmer's wife's mouth hung open in astonishment.

The monk reached up and broke off a tree branch to use as a walking stick. Then he clapped his hands sharply, and the tree vanished.

Everyone cheered.

The monk bowed to everyone and limped away with the help of his new walking stick.

The farmer's wife turned to her cart, ready to shout out that her sweet pears were for sale. But they were all gone. And the cart's wooden handle had disappeared.

"That monk did this!" she cried out.

But it was too late. The monk was nowhere to be found.

A TAOIST STORY

Taoism is one of China's ancient religions. In China and among Chinese people around the world, Taoism is practised through ancestor worship, fortune-telling, Chinese medicine, feng-shui and qigong meditation. Other expressions of Taoism are found in the martial arts and the world of ghosts.

Taoism encourages people to be humble and generous. It points to nature for guidance, seeking ways for us to be in harmony with the universe. Long ago, people believed that Taoist priests had secret powers, like living to a very old age and repelling evil spirits that could cause trouble.

A CHINESE PROVERB:

樹倒猢猻散

Translation: A tree tumbles; the monkeys scatter.

Meaning: After someone loses power, his or her followers will vanish.

Almond Jelly with Fresh Fruit

鮮果杏仁豆腐

One of the few traditional Chinese desserts is almond jelly—also known as almond float. My cousins in Hawaii introduced me to this recipe. Like the monk in this story, sharing this humble yet delightful dessert will bring you friends who appreciate your generosity.

INGREDIENTS

1	envelope	unflavored gelatin
¾	cup	water
⅓	cup	sugar
1 ¼	cups	whole milk
2	tsp	almond extract
2	tbsp	orange juice
2	cups	fresh fruit, such as berries, peaches or pears

Note: Fresh pineapple, kiwi fruit, papayas, honeydew, figs and ginger contain enzymes that will ruin the jelly. If you wish to use these fruits with the almond jelly, heat them to 185°F to destroy the enzyme.

EQUIPMENT

- measuring cups & spoons
- liquid measuring cups
- small pot
- wooden spoon
- rubber spatula
- 8-inch square glass or ceramic pan
- plastic wrap
- cutting board & knife

METHOD

1. In a liquid measuring cup or small bowl, soften gelatin in about ¼ cup of cold water until gelatin granules swell.

2. Meanwhile, in the pot over medium heat, heat ½ cup of water with the sugar and milk until sugar dissolves. Stir with the wooden spoon. Be careful not to scorch the milk.

3. Add the softened gelatin by scraping it out with the rubber spatula. Over a gentle heat, mix well to fully dissolve gelatin. Do not boil.

4. Remove from heat, and stir to cool.

5. Add the almond extract and blend in evenly.

6. Pour into the 8-inch square pan.

7. Chill in the refrigerator for 3 hours, or until firm.

8. Meanwhile, wash fresh fruit in cold water, and remove any blemishes. Peel. Cut into bite-sized pieces. Pour orange juice over fruit, and stir to coat. Refrigerate until ready to use.

9. When almond jelly is firm, cut into ¾-inch cubes.

10. Spoon about ¾ cup of almond jelly cubes into individual serving bowls, with a generous scoop of fresh fruit.

11. Serve immediately and enjoy!

Magic Rice on the Mountain

山上神米

Long ago in China, there lived a widow and her little
girl, Lan-fen. The widow grew rice in her field,
and every year, under gentle rains, she planted and
harvested two crops. Lan-fen grew strong and tall in the
warm sunshine. As the widow worked, she sang a happy
song:

> *Up at dawn to work the land,*
> *Not afraid of a dirty hand.*
> *Going home to feed my girl,*
> *After food, we'll dance and whirl.*

At the start of the season, the widow bent over and
pressed seedlings into the mud, one by one. It was back-
breaking work. When the rice stalks ripened, she bent
over and cut them, handful by handful.

In the kitchen, Lan-fen washed the rice with care, and
never let a single grain float away. She knew to eat every
grain of rice in her bowl.

Her mother smiled and sang:

*Mother and daughter always together
In storms or sun, no matter the weather.*

One dark night, bandits raided the village for food and slaves. Next morning, Lan-fen couldn't find her mother anywhere.

Lan-fen went to stay with her uncle, the schoolmaster. He lived in a run-down house in town. He had few students so his classroom was thick with dust and cobwebs.

Lan-fen helped her uncle as much as she could. She swept the floors and aired his blankets. She cleaned his smoking pipes and made cloth buttons to sell.

But the uncle worried that Lan-fen ate too much at meals. He put out smaller and smaller bowls of rice, but she never complained that she was hungry.

"Useless girl," he grumbled. "She is a hole in my money box!"

The neighbors adored the girl and watched her closely, so the uncle could do nothing to harm her.

One day, the uncle took Lan-fen to a mountain-top temple. It was a long trip, so she brought along her bowl and chopsticks.

Along the way, she picked flowers and poked at insects. The higher they went, the fewer the trees.

Soon the land was barren and rocks covered the ground everywhere.

"I must go visit a friend," the uncle said. "Wait for me here."

"Is there anything to eat?" Lan-fen asked.

"Fill your bowl with white stones," he replied. "The mountain is full of them."

"How shall I cook them?" she asked.

"With your feet. Rub them together to make heat." Then off he went, scowling.

Lan-fen sat and sang the song from her mother.

Mother and daughter always together
In storms or sun, no matter the weather.

Eight days and eight nights later, the uncle finally returned. He didn't expect to see Lan-fen alive. *She should have starved to death—or wild animals should have devoured her.*

Instead, her happy voice called out, "Uncle, you are so wise! I filled my bowl with white stones. I sang, and soon they turned into grains of rice. Then I rubbed my feet together and put them around my bowl. In an instant, fluffy hot rice was ready!"

So they went down, down, down the mountain and back to town. She told her story to the neighbors, but they all shook their heads. No one believed white stones could turn into rice.

Weeks later, the uncle went up the mountain again with Lan-fen and her bowl and chopsticks. Along the way, she picked flowers and poked at insects. Along the way, her uncle scowled and cursed. Higher and higher they went.

Lan-fen felt hungry, so she filled her bowl with white stones.

"Come here," her uncle called from the edge of the cliff.

"Yes, Uncle."

When she got close, he grabbed the bowl and threw it over the edge. "Your magic is evil!"

He stormed down the mountain leaving her behind.

Lan-fen peered over the edge. To her surprise, the bowl was floating below, atop a lotus leaf. They flew up and came to rest at her feet.

She sang her mother's song, and again the stones turned into grains of raw rice:

Mother and daughter always together
In storms or sun, no matter the weather.

Just then, a monk walked by.

"This is a miracle," he exclaimed. He took Lan-fen and the bowl to the temple, and put the grains of wondrous rice in a golden box. Then he sent her down, down, down the mountain. "Hurry home to your village. This is your lucky day."

When she walked through the rice fields, she found her mother waiting in front of their old house.

Mother and daughter embraced.

"Didn't I say that we would always be together?" said the widow. "The bandits took me far away and sold me as a servant. But my new owner let me go."

Soon people from far and near heard about the wondrous rice kept in the golden box in the temple atop the mountain. On hearing Lan-fen's story, they smiled to remember mothers and daughters everywhere and all the farm-workers who grew food.

Her uncle visited the temple too, but when he heard the story of Lan-fen, his face darkened. He waited until night and stole the golden box with the grains of wondrous rice. Then he headed down, down, down the mountain to his shabby home in town.

He boiled some water, cooked the rice and ate his fill. Then he lay down. He had hardly fallen asleep when he screamed as sharp pains ripped through his stomach.

The wondrous rice had turned back into stones!

OLD STORY PATTERN

Orphans are found in many folktales. They are a kind of a hero with many disadvantages. The orphan not only lacks parents, but also encounters great dangers. Because the orphan is a child, she is seen to be innocent, but the adult world around her is usually dark and evil. To make things worse, the orphan is often tricked or betrayed by an adult caregiver whom she trusts.

SACRED MOUNTAINS IN CHINA

In Chinese stories, mountains are seen as magical places. In early tales, the mountains were seen as great pillars holding up the heavens, keeping them from falling onto the earth. The tops of mountains were often thought of as gateways into heaven—the home of the gods.

Many legends involve hermits who live high up in mountain caves hidden in deep forests. These wise men knew how to live in harmony with nature.

In both the Taoist and Buddhist religions, many temples were built in the mountains to honor spirits and gods. These temples served as retreats where people could come to escape the turmoil of life in busy towns.

Artists also went to the mountains to find inspiration for their writing and painting. Chinese paintings often feature mountains that loom large over the landscape.

In Chinese martial-arts stories and movies, the schools where the heroes are taught how to fight are usually high up in the mountains.

In Chinese mythology, when gods traveled, often it was a magic lotus flower that lifted them up into and through the air.

A CHINESE PROVERB

生米煮成熟飯

Translation: Raw grains cooked into rice.

Meaning: Some things cannot be undone.

Fried Rice

炒飯

When I was growing up, steamed rice was always served with meals. Fried rice was served on special occasions such as a ten-course banquet. This recipe is a great way to use up leftover cooked rice, vegetables and bits of meat. These leftovers can be transformed into a delicious new dish of fried rice, just like the white stones magically turned into rice for Lan-fen.

INGREDIENTS

2-3		large eggs
5	cups	cold cooked rice
1	tbsp	peanut or canola oil
¾	tsp	salt
1	cup	frozen peas
1	cup	diced char-siu (Chinese BBQ pork) or ham
3		green onions, thinly sliced
1	tsp	sesame oil (optional)

EQUIPMENT

- measuring cups & spoons
- cutting board & chef's knife
- small bowl & fork
- wok or dutch oven
- wooden spoon

METHOD

1. In the small bowl, lightly beat the eggs with the fork.

2. Loosen the cold cooked rice with a fork so it is not clumped together.

3. Heat the wok or dutch oven over high heat until a drop of water sizzles and evaporates. Add the peanut or canola oil, and swirl to coat the cooking surface.

4. Add the lightly beaten eggs, and swirl to create a thin layer. Cook for 30-60 seconds.

5. Add the cooked rice and salt while stir-frying and breaking up the eggs with the wooden spoon. Stir-fry the rice mixture for 1-2 minutes. Then add the frozen peas and diced pork or ham, stirring until the rice is hot (3-5 minutes).

6. When all the ingredients are evenly heated, add the green onions and sesame oil (if desired), and stir-fry until well distributed.

7. Serve immediately and enjoy the magic.

VARIATION

1. The pork can be substituted with diced cooked chicken or cooked small shrimp.

2. For a vegetarian option, omit meat and increase the eggs to 3 or 4.

The Schoolmaster's Autumn Festival
老師慶中秋

One day, Schoolmaster Chang hurried along a country road, humming to himself. He had spent several weeks teaching in town, and now he was heading home to his village to celebrate the Autumn Festival.

A monk walked back and forth in front of a roadside temple, moaning and rubbing his head as if he were in great pain.

"What is wrong, honorable sir?" asked the schoolmaster. "What makes you so sad?"

The monk pointed to the roof of the temple. "The tiles have fallen down and broken into pieces. We have no money to buy new tiles and fix the hole."

"Here, take my silver. The temple must be kept dry."

Schoolmaster Chang went on his way. Soon he came upon an elderly woman weeping bitterly.

"Why, Granny Ling, whatever is the matter?"

"I am so sad. I cannot pay the landlord, and he is about to seize my farm."

"Please, take these coins and pay him. You can repay me later when your crops are harvested."

Granny Ling thanked him and hurried away.

Finally Schoolmaster Chang reached his village. In front of his neighbor's house, the twin boys were crying.

"Is there something wrong, little ones?" he asked. "You mustn't be sad during the Autumn Festival."

"We made lanterns from bamboo and paper, for the parade," said one twin.

"But Ma has no money," said his brother, "to buy candles."

"Here, take my last coins and go buy some candles."

When Schoolmaster Chang walked into his house, his wife looked worried. She asked, "How much money did you bring home?"

"I have nothing."

Her eyebrows flew up in surprise. "What?"

"I gave silver to a monk. The roof of the temple needed to be fixed. Then I gave money to Granny Ling—otherwise the landlord was going to seize her farm."

"You know that I have to eat for two to feed the baby in my belly. Surely you must have a few coins left."

The schoolmaster hung his head. "I gave my last coins to our neighbor's twin boys. They needed to buy candles for their Autumn Festival lanterns."

When the teacher and his wife went to bed, they tossed and turned. They couldn't sleep because they were so hungry.

In the middle of the night, the wife sat up. "Why don't

you go and dig up some sweet potatoes from Widow Lu's field?"

"But her son, Little Ming, will be guarding them."

"He's a growing boy. I promise you he will be fast asleep."

"But I tell my students that it is wrong to steal."

"You are a teacher, but you are also a husband. You shouldn't have given away all your money."

"I'll ask the Earth God what to do," Schoolmaster Chang said, getting out of bed.

The Earth God will never allow him to steal, she thought. *I need to do something.* "While you go and fetch the pitchfork," she told him, "I will light the candle on the shrine."

After lighting the candle, the schoolmaster's wife crept under the table of the shrine.

The teacher lay down the pitchfork and knelt in front of the statue of the Earth God. "Mighty God, please give me advice," he whispered, raising his hands and closing his eyes in prayer. "I gave away my money just before the Autumn Festival. I have no money to feed my family and no money to celebrate. Will you allow me to dig up a few sweet potatoes from Widow Lu's field?"

Then he closed his eyes, took two charms from the table and dropped them onto the floor. Each charm had one round side and one flat side. The two charms landed with both round sides facing up. That meant the god's answer was no. But before he could open his eyes, Schoolmaster Chang's wife reached out and flipped over one of the charms.

"Thank you, mighty God," he cried. "Thank you for giving me permission to dig up the sweet potatoes. I promise to repay Widow Lu as soon as I earn some money."

He went to the field, and just as his wife had promised, Widow Lu's son was fast asleep. So the schoolmaster dug up a few of her sweet potatoes and hurried home.

Next morning, Widow Lu saw that her field had been dug up. She yanked Little Ming by the ear and shouted, "You lazy boy. You were supposed to guard our field!"

Widow Lu spent the day searching the village to find out who had stolen her sweet potatoes. When she passed the teacher's house, a familiar aroma drifted out.

"Ahhh! It is Schoolmaster Chang who stole my sweet potatoes!"

She burst into their house and dragged him into the street, shouting, "You stole sweet potatoes from me!"

The villagers came running to see what the fuss was all about.

Widow Lu shouted, "You, a man of learning, stealing from my field!"

"Shame on you!" shouted the angry villagers.

"I asked the Earth God if I could take them," the schoolmaster pleaded. "And he said yes."

"Our Earth God would never tell anyone to steal!" the farmers shouted. They threw clods of dirt at him.

"I promised to repay Widow Lu as soon as I could," the teacher added, holding up his hands to protect himself.

"You are a thief and a liar!" the farmers shouted.

"No!" a voice shouted out. "Schoolmaster Chang is a good man." Granny Ling stepped forward and told how he had helped her with money just yesterday.

Then the twins from next door spoke up. "Schoolmaster Chang is a generous man. Yesterday, he gave us money to buy candles for our Autumn Festival lanterns."

The monk came forward and held up his hands. "Schoolmaster Chang is a kind man. He gave me money to buy tiles to fix the temple roof."

Finally Schoolmaster Chang's wife cried out, "I told him to dig up the sweet potatoes. I am with child." Then she confessed how she had switched the charms.

Granny Ling went to Widow Lu and said, "My good woman, I lent you some seeds for your field. How could you be so mean?"

Widow Lu dipped her head in shame.

The twins from next door went to Little Ming, and said, "Do you remember when we helped you weed your field so you could go fishing with us?"

Lastly, the monk spoke to Widow Lu, "Schoolmaster Chang has said he will repay you for what he has taken."

"There is no need for him to repay me," she replied. "He has already paid for them through his kindness and generosity. And there will be plenty of sweet potatoes for everyone at the Autumn Festival."

The villagers cheered and everyone went home to bring food to Schoolmaster Chang and his wife. That way, everyone celebrated the Autumn Festival that year.

AN OLD STORY FROM THE STAGE

This story is a re-telling of the Chinese opera Scholar Xia's New Year. During festivals, everyone would gather to watch operas. In these performances, the forces of good always won over the forces of evil, and ideals such as duty and loyalty were extolled.

EDUCATED FOLK

Scholars appeared in many Chinese stories. Educated people were much respected in China because it was believed that anyone from a humble background could improve the family's position through education.

AUTUMN FESTIVAL

The festival in this story was the annual celebration held by farmers to mark the end of the harvest. It always occurred on the 15th day of the eighth month of the lunar calendar, the same day as the autumn equinox, when the moon appears at its fullest—the harvest moon. During the autumn festival, people young and old gathered to admire the moon, light paper lanterns and feast on mooncakes.

A POTATO WITH A TALE

People in South America were the first to grow sweet potatoes for food over five thousand years ago. It is said that this food reached China in the middle of the Ming dynasty (AD 1368–1644) when a Chinese doctor traveled to Vietnam to work. When he returned to China, he smuggled out a sweet potato. A guard at the border caught him, but allowed him to take it home because the doctor had once cured him.

A CHINESE PROVERB

書 中 有 金 玉

Translation: *Books contain gold and jade.*

Meaning: *Education can bring you a good future.*

Roasted Sweet Potatoes

烤紅薯

The sweet potato is believed to have arrived in China from South America in the fifteenth century. Slow roasted sweet potatoes are widely enjoyed in China. Today, roasted vegetables are as popular as the roasted sweet potatoes made by the schoolmaster's wife.

INGREDIENTS

1	lb	sweet potatoes (or yams or both)
1	tbsp	vegetable oil such as canola or corn oil
1	tsp	pure sesame oil
¼	tsp	salt
¼	tsp	five-spice powder, or white or Sichuan pepper
1	tsp	sesame seeds (optional)

DIP

⅓	cup	light mayonnaise
1	tsp	fresh ginger, minced
1	tsp	green onions, finely chopped
¼	tsp	sweet-chilli or garlic-chilli sauce (to taste)

EQUIPMENT

- measuring spoons
- cutting board
- chef's knife
- 2 small bowls
- rimmed baking sheet
- egg lifter
- oven mitts

METHOD

1. Adjust oven rack to the middle of the oven. Preheat the oven to 400°F.

2. Wash and scrub sweet potatoes.

3. Cut sweet potatoes into lengths, ½-inch thick.

4. In a small bowl, combine the vegetable oil with the sesame oil. In the other, combine the salt with the five-spice powder.

5. On the rimmed baking sheet, toss the sweet potato lengths with the combined oils to evenly coat. Then sprinkle the salt and five-spice powder mixture evenly over the coated sweet potatoes. Toss again to combine. Arrange the sweet potatoes in a single layer. If desired, sprinkle sesame seeds on top.

6. Bake in the hot oven for 20–30 minutes. After 12 minutes, toss and turn the sweet potatoes and continue baking. Repeat, tossing again as needed to ensure even browning. The sweet potatoes are ready when easily pierced with a fork.

7. Transfer the sweet potatoes with an egg lifter to a serving dish.

8. Serve warm as is or with the dip, made by combining the dip ingredients in a small serving bowl.

Monkey Fights White Bone

孫悟空三打白骨精

Long ago, a monk and his disciples Monkey, Pig and Friar traveled over the mountains to India to find the holy books of Buddhism and bring them to China. Monkey was smart and loyal, and Pig was jealous of Monkey. They often fought and argued.

At White Tiger Hill, the monk told Monkey to get some food. Monkey leapt onto a cloud and saw a speck of red in the distance. He told the monk, "Master, there are ripe peaches on a faraway hillside. I'll fetch some." And off he went.

Meanwhile, White Bone, the witch of White Tiger Hill, caught sight of the monk.

If only I can taste his flesh, she thought, *then I can live forever.* She quickly transformed herself into a pretty maiden and went up to the travelers.

"Young miss, good afternoon," Pig said. "What do you carry in your basket?"

"Steamed rice and vegetables."

"Young miss, why are you in this forest?" the monk asked. "It is not safe here."

"I'm delivering this food to my husband, who's

working in the fields. You must be hungry. Please take some of this food for yourselves."

"No, we cannot accept," the monk said. "Your husband will be hungry."

My master is a fool not to take the food, Pig thought.

At that moment, Monkey returned with the peaches. Right away he saw through the witch's disguise. "Master, that's White Bone! She's a witch," he said, lashing out with his fighting stick.

The maiden dropped her basket and fell dead to the ground. The witch flew away, unharmed.

"Monkey, how dare you?" the monk said. "Buddhism allows no killing, not even of animals. Why were you so quick to lash out at that poor girl?"

"Master, that girl is but an illusion, the product of White Bone's magic."

Jealous of Monkey, Pig pointed to her still body and said, "Master, Monkey has gone against our principles. He killed that poor girl."

Friar didn't want to get involved, so he said nothing.

Who should I believe? the monk thought. *Monkey or Pig?*

"Monkey, it was wrong to kill. You must leave us."

"Master, don't let Pig trick you."

Meanwhile, White Bone had transformed herself into an old woman as frail and wrinkled as a dried leaf. Clutching a cane, she tottered up, calling, "Daughter, where are you? Daughter, I see your food basket, but where are you?"

"Master, look, the girl's mother has come," Pig said.

"Nonsense!" Monkey said. "Can't you see that she's too old to be the girl's mother?" And he immediately struck White Bone with his fighting stick.

The old woman dropped to the ground, dead, and the witch flew away.

The monk was horrified. "Look what you've done, Monkey. Now you really must go away."

"But, Master, I've only been trying to protect you."

White Bone wanted immortality more than anything. So she came back as a white-bearded old man carrying prayer beads. He limped over to the monk.

"Have you seen my dear wife and my beloved daughter?"

"I fear they have been killed," the monk said sadly.

But Monkey was not fooled. He immediately struck out with his fighting stick, and the old man fell to the ground with a thud. The witch flew away.

"Violence is against our principles, Master," Pig said.

"He's right," Friar said.

"My decision is final," the monk said. "Go."

Monkey flew out over the clouds, landing on Flower Fruit Mountain, his faraway home. But Monkey could not relax. *Without me,* he thought, *my Master is in danger.*

The monk and his two remaining disciples carried on through the mountain pass until night fell.

"Look, a temple," Pig said, pointing ahead. "We can shelter there tonight. Maybe there's food."

The three travelers opened the great front doors of the temple and walked in.

"This is a strange place," Friar said. "There are no priests."

Soon they reached a grand hall, covered in dust and cobwebs and surrounded by statues of gods.

The travelers walked up to the altar.

All of a sudden the statues turned into leaping, screaming demons, urged on by White Bone.

Pig managed to hide, but the demons captured the monk and Friar, and tied them up.

"This is no temple!" Friar shouted. "It's a cave of demons."

I must do something, Pig thought in his hiding place. *Monkey can help.*

So Pig sneaked out of the cave, leapt onto a cloud and flew to Flower Fruit Mountain.

"Monkey, White Bone has captured our master and Friar!"

"Pig, you betrayed me. Why should I help you?" Monkey shook his head in anger, and looked away. "Master should have believed me, not you."

"Then I will fight the demons myself!" Pig roared. "I am not afraid!"

He went back to the temple and smashed his way past the guards. He fought bravely, but was captured and tied up.

"Ha! Now I will invite my mother, Grand Dame, to feast on your flesh," White Bone said to the monk, "and we both will live forever."

Meanwhile, back on Flower Fruit Mountain, Monkey was having second thoughts. *Stupid Pig will never defeat White Bone.*

So he leapt up into the clouds and flew back and forth until he saw Grand Dame and her followers on White Tiger Hill. They were heading for the demon cave. He swooped down and killed them. Then he disguised himself as Grand Dame.

When Grand Dame greeted White Bone, the demons danced and clapped. Grand Dame walked over to Monk, and asked, "Where is Monkey?"

"I cast him out. He killed three people. Buddhists respect life, unlike you demons."

"You are a fool," White Bone said. Then she twitched and turned into the young girl with the basket of food.

The demons danced and shouted with glee.

Then she twitched again and turned into the old woman.

The demons hooted and stamped their feet.

Then she twitched again and turned into the old man with the prayer beads.

The demons somersaulted in the air.

"Monkey was right," the monk said. "I should have listened to him."

"You still can," Monkey said, reverting to his true form and taking up a battle stance with his fighting stick.

White Bone and her demons were no match for Monkey. He killed them all, and released Pig, Friar and the monk from their bonds.

"I knew all along you would rescue us," Friar said.

"I never doubted you," Pig said.

And I'll never trust you, Pig, thought Monkey.

"The road to India is long," the monk said. "We must leave immediately."

A FAMOUS NOVEL

In the year AD 630, a monk named Xuanzang walked from China through today's Kyrgyzstan, Uzbekistan and Afghanistan to reach India. He toured holy places in India for 13 years and then took home many Buddhist texts that were later translated. This story is an excerpt from a sixteenth-century Chinese novel, Journey to the West, *inspired by the famous journey.*

The story of the monk follows the archetype of the quest—the Quest Pattern—where the hero takes a long journey, meeting many dangers along the way. After much hard work and sacrifice, he returns home, older and wiser.

In Journey to the West, *the monk is captured by demons many times, but is saved by his three guards, the great warriors Monkey, Pig and Friar. The four travelers argue and fight among themselves, much like ordinary people.*

The novel enjoyed great popularity in China for centuries, and the story has been told in many forms—operas, stage plays, movies, TV series, animated cartoons and comic books.

NOT EATING MEAT

One rule in Buddhism is "do not kill." This led many people to stop eating meat. Even before Buddhism reached China, many Chinese people did not eat meat or drink wine, for religious reasons.

There are two Chinese terms for vegetarian food: zhai-cai 齋菜, pronounced jai sai, and su-cai 素菜, pronounced soo sai. Doufu, known as tofu in the West, is made from soybeans, and provides non-meat protein for many vegetarians.

Crisp Tofu and Stir-Fried Bok-Choy
青菜豆腐

Vegetarian meals are common in China due to the influence of Buddhism, which respects life for all living creatures. Meat can be replaced by protein-rich soy products such as bean curd—also known as tofu. I am sure that Pig, Monkey, Friar and Monk would find this dish of crisp tofu and stir-fried baby bok-choy over rice a very satisfying and delicious meal.

INGREDIENTS

1	lb	medium-firm tofu
¼	cup	cornstarch
¼	cup	peanut or canola oil

GLAZE FOR TOFU

1 ½	tbsp	soy sauce
1 ½	tbsp	granulated sugar
3	tbsp	vegetable or chicken stock or liquid from dried mushrooms

VEGETABLES

½	lb	baby bok-choy or baby Shanghai bok-choy
3-4		dried shiitake mushrooms
1		medium carrot, peeled
1		red bell pepper
2	tbsp	fresh ginger, shredded or minced
2		medium garlic cloves, minced
2		green onions, thinly sliced on a diagonal

SAUCE

½	cup	vegetable or chicken stock or liquid from dried mushrooms
1	tbsp	oyster sauce
2	tsp	soy sauce
2	tsp	cornstarch
1	tsp	sesame oil

EQUIPMENT

- 2 dinner plates
- measuring spoons
- liquid measure
- cutting board
- chef's knife
- paper towels

- colander
- vegetable peeler
- 3 small bowls
- 12-inch skillet
- tongs
- spatula

METHOD

1. Remove tofu from its packaging and drain well. Place directly on paper towels to absorb excess moisture. Let sit for 15-30 minutes.

2. Meanwhile, wash all vegetables thoroughly. Drain well in a colander. Trim the stem ends of bok-choy for an easier and more thorough cleaning.

3. In a small bowl of hot water, soak the dried shiitake mushrooms until soft (15-20 minutes). Then squeeze excess water out of the mushrooms. Save all mushroom liquid for sauce. Cut off the mushroom stem ends and discard. Then slice the mushroom caps into ¼-inch slices.

4. Slice the carrot on a diagonal about ¼-inch thick. Slice the pepper into ¼-inch strips after removing the seed pod and stem.

5. In a small bowl, combine the ingredients for the glaze. In another bowl combine the sauce ingredients. Set aside.

6. Cut tofu into 1-inch cubes.

7. Heat 2 tbsp peanut or canola oil in the skillet over medium heat, until the oil ripples but does not smoke. Dredge the tofu pieces in cornstarch and shake off excess. For best results, coat tofu in cornstarch just before cooking. Using the tongs, carefully place half of the coated tofu pieces into the hot oil. Cook until golden brown on all sides. When the tofu is golden, carefully remove with the tongs and place on fresh paper towels to drain excess oil. Add another tablespoon of oil as needed before cooking the remaining half of the tofu cubes.

8. When all the tofu pieces have been fried, drain any remaining cooking oil from the skillet. Wipe the skillet clean. Return the crisp tofu cubes to skillet and add the glaze ingredients. Cook over medium heat while gently tossing the tofu cubes until evenly glazed. Remove and set aside on a plate.

9. Wipe skillet clean and heat one more tablespoon of oil over medium heat. When the oil is hot, stir in the garlic and ginger for about 15 seconds to flavor the oil. Add the carrot, pepper and mushroom slices, and stir to coat them with the flavored oil. Then add the baby bok-choy and stir quickly to lightly wilt the greens. Cover the skillet for a few minutes until the vegetables are tender-crisp. Then remove the lid.

10. Return the glazed tofu cubes to the skillet with the vegetables. Stir the sauce mixture before adding to a well in the middle of the tofu mixture. Cook, stirring, until the sauce is slightly thickened and no longer milky. Add the green onions.

11. Transfer to a serving platter. Can be enjoyed with steamed rice.

Steamed Bread and Salt

饅頭與鹽

Long, long ago, there lived a small family with only a brother, a sister and their mother. Sister stayed home with Mother, weaving cloth to sell. Brother was an important merchant and lived in a grand mansion on an island off the coast. He rarely called on Mother. He was too busy.

One summer, the price of cloth dropped so low that Mother and Sister couldn't afford to buy food.

"Go ask Brother for some steamed bread," Mother said, "and tell him to call on me."

"He won't help us," said Sister. "When Brother became rich, he forgot all about us."

"It's his birthday. He'll be generous today. Here's some money for the ferry."

At Brother's mansion, wealthy guests came to offer him warm wishes. His guards wouldn't let Sister in, but by pretending to be the maidservant of a guest, she slipped in.

A feast was underway. Sweet aromas wafted from roasted meats. Vegetables of green, red and purple were cooked to perfection. Fried rice and long-life noodles

filled giant platters. The guests shouted and played games over cups of wine.

Sister sneaked over to Brother, and whispered, "Mother wants you to call on her. We have no money for food, now that the price of cloth has dropped so low."

Brother sent Sister to the kitchen to eat with the servants. When she finished eating, the cook gave her two pieces of steamed bread and showed her to the back door. Sister hurried toward home.

An old woman squatting on the dock called out, "Young miss, do you have food to spare?"

"I only have two pieces of steamed bread."

"I am so hungry. Can you spare one piece?"

I have already eaten. I can surely spare one piece. So she unwrapped the bread and gave one piece to the old woman.

"Young miss, thank you for this. But my husband is hungry too."

"This piece is for my mother."

"Surely she would share."

She's right. So she followed the old woman to her nearby hut.

"I smell steamed bread!" a voice called out.

A blind man was sitting at a table next to four brocade boxes.

When Sister handed him the bread, he pushed forward the boxes. "One of these boxes is for you. Please choose one for yourself."

"There is no need for a gift in return."

But the old man insisted that she open the boxes. Each box was lined with silk. One had a pair of silver chopsticks, another had two golden spoons, another had four jade cups, and in the last box was a stone mortar and pestle.

We already have chopsticks, spoons and cups, she thought. *But we don't have anything to grind our salt and spices.* "I'll take the mortar and pestle. Thank you so much."

"A wise choice," the blind man said. "The mortar and pestle is magic."

"If you tap it three times and say, 'serve some salt, serve some salt,' the bowl will fill with salt," the old woman said.

"Now I must hurry and catch the ferry," the young girl said, rushing out. "Good bye, and thank you again."

The old woman ran after her and pulled her sleeve. "When you want it to stop, say, 'save some salt, save some salt.'"

When Sister got home, Mother asked, "Did your brother give us any food?"

"His cook fed me and gave us steamed bread."

"Then we must thank your brother. Where is the steamed bread?"

"I gave it to an old woman and her blind husband. They were so hungry."

"But we have nothing to eat! Was that a wise choice?"

"They gave us a gift." Sister held out the mortar and pestle. "This has magical powers."

"Magical powers?"

"Watch." Sister tapped the mortar three times using the pestle, and then called out, "Serve some salt, serve some salt."

White salt filled the little bowl and began pouring out. Sister ran for a sack. When it was full, she tapped the mortar three times again, and said, "Save some salt, save some salt." The salt stopped pouring out.

Mother clapped her hands and laughed. "Take the salt and sell it at the market. With the money, buy flour for steamed bread, and meat and vegetables to go with it."

So Sister took the salt and sold it at the market. From then on, mother and daughter didn't have to make cloth. With the money they earned from selling salt, they made steamed bread and shared it with their neighbors. They had plenty of money left over to buy new chairs for their little house. For the first time ever, it looked warm and cozy.

"You must go soon to thank your brother," said Mother.

Sister nodded.

One day while Sister was at the market, Brother came to the house. When he saw how cozy the house was, he said, "Why

Mother, you've bought new furniture. Your cloth must be selling well."

"We don't have to make cloth anymore. We sell salt now."
"Salt?"
"Yes, salt. We have you to thank for all this."
"Me?"
"Yes, you. After you gave Sister steamed bread to bring home, she gave it to a hungry old woman and her blind husband."
"So?"
Mother pointed to the mortar and pestle. "The blind man gave her this mortar and pestle in return. If we tap three times and say, 'serve some salt, serve some salt,' salt pours out."

I'll sell the salt myself and make lots more money, thought Brother. He grabbed the mortar and pestle and ran away, hurrying to the ferry.

In his cabin on the ferry, Brother thought, *Let's see if this thing works.* He tapped the little bowl three times and called out, "Serve some salt, serve some salt."

White salt spewed out from the mortar, and he roared with pleasure.

Salt poured out faster and faster. Soon it covered Brother's feet.

Concerned, Brother tapped the mortar three times and called out, "Stop the salt, stop the salt."

But the salt kept pouring out. It came up to his knees and filled his boots.

"No more salt, no more salt!" he shouted.

But the salt kept pouring out. Soon it came up to his waist and filled his pockets. Salt flowed under the door of the cabin and onto the deck.

"Sir, the boat is tipping," the ferry boat captain said, pounding on the cabin door. "Open up, sir! What are you doing in there?"

"Slow down salt, slow down salt!" Brother screamed. But salt continued to pour, and now rose over the bulkhead. The sailors jumped overboard and swam away. The captain followed. Brother tried to jump too, but the salt weighed him down. He couldn't move. He screamed for help, to no avail.

Finally the ferry boat sank and took Brother down to the bottom of the sea. Luckily for Mother and Sister, Brother had no other heirs, so they went to live in the big house on the island.

To this day, the mortar continues to pour salt into the ocean, making it salty.

OLD STORY PATTERN

There are folktales from all around the world that explain why the sea is salty. Like the story of Steamed Bread and Salt, many of them involve some magical device that spews out salt from the ocean floor.

Many folktales describe kind-hearted people who do good deeds in helping the less fortunate. They may feed a hungry beggar or save the life of an animal being chased by a hunter. These generous folk are then rewarded by a flow of riches that never ends—food or gold coins might burst out of the ground, or overflow from a magic cooking pot.

These stories often end with a look at the other side of kindness. When a greedy or selfish person grabs hold of the magic device to gain its flow of riches, terrible things happen to him or her. In this Chinese story, Brother is a bad person not just because he is greedy, but also because he fails to show respect to his mother.

A CHINESE PROVERB

飲 水 思 源

Translation: *Drink water, think of the (water) spring.*

Meaning: *Never forget the source of one's happiness.*

CHINESE BREADS

There are two popular kinds of bread in China—bread made without rising, like the Mexican tortilla or Indian chapati, called bing 餅, and puffy buns made from risen dough, called bao-zi 包子. There are many kinds of bing and bao-zi, both sweet and savory. Man-tou 饅頭is another name for steamed buns, and usually refers to buns with no filling inside.

In China, bread is made in portions small enough for one person.

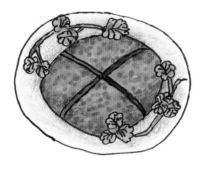

Man-Tou (Steamed Bread)

清蒸饅頭

One of my favorite treats from Chinatown bakeries is steamed buns. They can be filled (bao-zi)—either savory or sweet. Or they can be plain (man-tou), and used to scoop up delicious sauces during meals. This is a traditional way of eating in northern China, where wheat rather than rice is grown. Make sure you have several hours to devote to this recipe, as the dough needs rising time.

INGREDIENTS

1	cup	warm water (110°F)
2	tsp	sugar
1	pkg	dried traditional yeast (2 ¼ tsp)
2	tbsp	vegetable oil
½	tsp	salt
3	tbsp	sugar
3 ¼	cups	unbleached flour
½	tsp	sesame oil

EQUIPMENT

- measuring cups & spoons
- liquid measuring cup
- large mixing bowl
- wooden spoon
- plastic wrap
- tea towels
- parchment paper
- chef's knife
- dutch oven
- steaming rack
- shallow heatproof dish

METHOD

1. Warm the liquid measuring cup and large mixing bowl with hot tap water, and drain well. This helps to keep the yeast warm and promote its growth. Measure the warm water into the bowl. Add the 2 tsp sugar and stir to dissolve. Then sprinkle in the dried yeast. Let sit in a warm draft-free spot for 10-15 minutes to allow the yeast to ferment. When ready, a bubbly foam will appear on the top.

2. Stir in the vegetable oil, salt, 3 tbsp sugar and flour with a wooden spoon until the dough is formed and holds together. Knead the dough on a lightly floured surface for about 8–10 minutes until the dough is smooth and elastic.

3. Lightly grease the large bowl with the sesame oil, and place the dough back in. Cover with plastic wrap, then a tea towel. Let the dough rise in a warm place until it has doubled in volume (about 1 hour and 15 minutes).

4. Meanwhile cut parchment paper into twelve 2 ½-inch squares.

5. Punch the dough down with your fist to deflate. Then roll the dough into a log and cut into 12 equal pieces. Shape one piece of dough at a time and keep the rest of the dough pieces covered to prevent from drying out. To shape, slightly flatten each round of dough with your hand and then gather the edges together and twist. Place, twisted side down, and gently roll the ball of dough under your cupped hand to get a smooth surface. Place parchment paper on a baking sheet, then dough on top of parchment square. Cover shaped

dough with a tea towel. Repeat with remaining pieces of dough, placing them about 2 inches apart. Let the shaped dough rise in a warm place for about 30-45 minutes, until they are light and puffy.

6. Bring water to a gentle boil in the dutch oven. Place steaming rack in the bottom of the pot. On top of the rack, place the heatproof dish and fill with as many buns as the dish will hold in a single layer, allowing space for them to expand. Cover the pot and steam for about 15 minutes. Do not peek or remove the lid during this cooking time or the dough may collapse. Repeat this cooking process with the remaining pieces.

VARIATION: If you have Chinese sausage (lup-cheong), you can wrap the dough around the sausage and steam it—making lup-cheong-bao!

Third Lady of Plank Bridge

板橋三娘

Late one afternoon long ago, a traveling merchant named Zhao found an inexpensive inn near Plank Bridge. The innkeeper was a woman named Third Lady. She showed him to a large room with six beds. "There is only one bed available—that one, on the far wall. The others have already been taken."

"The one by the door?"

"Yes. It leads to my room, but the door is locked and sealed. In the past these rooms were connected."

Zhao thanked her and placed his bag on the bed.

"It's dinnertime!" said Third Lady. "Come to the dining room as soon as you are ready."

When Zhao got there, it was filled with guests eating sumptuous dishes. "Please, Mr. Zhao, sit here and enjoy your meal," Third Lady said, holding out a chair next to a round table. "Tell me about the faraway places you have been to. I will never be able to travel the way you do."

A jug of wine was passed around as the guests shared their stories. "A toast to our new guest, Mr. Zhao!" said a plump white-haired gentleman, holding up a cup. Wine made Zhao drowsy, so he did not join in.

A bald man wearing a black silk jacket called out, "Third Lady, how many donkeys do you have now?"

"Too many to count," she replied. "Do you need one for your trip?"

Late into the evening, Third Lady bid her guests good night and poured them each another cup of wine. Then she went to her room.

The guests drank and joked some more, and soon they all went to bed.

Zhao could not fall asleep, no matter how he twisted and turned. *Will I ever fall asleep? I have a long way to go in the morning.*

Early in the morning, before the sun rose, he heard scratching sounds through the door next to his bed. Zhao tried to ignore them, but he couldn't. So he got up, knelt and peered through the keyhole. A single candle lit the room. He could just make out Third Lady taking clay figurines from a box—a man, an ox and a plough—and placing them onto the floor, which was pounded dirt. Then she sprinkled water over the figurines and clapped her hands twice.

To Zhao's amazement, the little statues came to life. The man urged the ox forward, and it pulled the plough, cutting furrows into the dirt.

Zhao pinched himself. *Am I dreaming?*

Then the tiny man scattered seeds, and Third Lady sprinkled water over the little farm.

Again she clapped her hands twice. Lo and behold, buckwheat sprang up right before Zhao's eyes. The seedlings grew into shoots, which became tall stalks.

The green field changed from red to brown. Finally, the little man harvested and winnowed the crop.

Third Lady clapped her hands again, and the man and the ox became still. Gently she put the clay figurines back into the box.

Then Third Lady ground the buckwheat into flour. She added salt, eggs and lard to make dough. By this time, it was nearly dawn. She formed the dough into little cakes, and smiled.

Zhao climbed into bed and shuddered. He hadn't slept a wink the entire night.

After the guests washed their faces and went to the dining room, Third Lady brought hot tea and buckwheat cakes. "Good morning, honored guests," she said. "Please eat these for breakfast before you go."

Zhao was too scared to eat anything. "Goodbye, everyone!" he shouted, rushing out the door.

When he got outside, he took a deep breath and peeked in through a side window. The guests were sipping their tea, talking and laughing. But as soon as they swallowed the buckwheat cakes, they dropped onto their hands and knees and turned into donkeys. Then Third Lady herded them out the back door and into the stable.

Zhao ran away as fast as he could. He told no one about what he had seen. *Who in the world would believe my story?*

Several weeks later, Zhao went back to the inn by Plank Bridge. This time he brought some buckwheat cakes that looked exactly like the ones that Third Lady had prepared in the middle of the night.

"Welcome, honored guest," Third Lady said. "You are just in time for dinner."

"I'm not feeling well," Zhao said. "I need rest."

When the other guests finished eating, they came into the room, got into their beds and fell fast asleep. Soon snores filled the room. Then Zhao heard Third Lady clap her hands twice. He was chilled to the bone.

When the sun rose, Zhao was the first to get up.

"Good morning, sir," Third Lady called out, coming in with breakfast for the guests. "The sky is blue. It is an excellent

day for travel. There are buckwheat cakes for breakfast. Please take some."

"Thank you, Third Lady," said Zhao, reaching for one. "They smell delicious!"

Third Lady smiled and turned to fetch the tea. Zhao quickly took out his own cakes and exchanged them for hers.

"Why, sir!" she exclaimed, pouring the tea. "You have not tasted my cake."

"Eat with me," he replied, returning her smile. "I brought some cakes with me. Please try one of mine while I try yours."

"Thank you, sir," she said, accepting it, not realizing that it was actually one of her own cakes. "You are truly a gentleman."

As soon as Third Lady bit into it, she fell onto her hands and knees and started to bray. An instant later, she turned into a donkey, and Zhao led her outside and rode off on her. "Now you will be able to travel far and wide."

Third Lady proved to be a strong and reliable beast. She could travel great distances each day without getting tired.

Several years went by. One day, as Zhao was leading Third Lady past a Buddhist temple, a priest saw them.

"Third Lady!" he called out, coming over and stroking the animal's ears. "What happened to you?" He turned to Zhao. "I think Third Lady has been punished enough." Then he placed his hand on the donkey's head and said, "You must never use your magic for evil again."

The donkey turned back into Third Lady. She ran into the bushes and was never seen again.

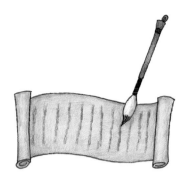

OLD STORY PATTERN

As well as being entertaining, many folktales also serve as warnings. A story such as Little Red Riding Hood *warns children to stay away from strangers. This tale of Third Lady warns travelers to be wary. It also has a Buddhist message, wherein Third Lady is forgiven.*

BUSINESS TRAVEL

The Silk Road connected China to Europe for over 3000 years. Stretching for 4000 miles, it began at the ancient Chinese capital of Xi'an and went through the deserts and mountains of Asia Minor, all the way to the Mediterranean. The caravans along the overland route used donkeys for carrying goods, because camels were too slow.

A CHINESE PROVERB

葉落歸根

Translation: *Falling leaves land near the roots.*

Meaning: *Remember your home when you are away.*

Green Onion Pancakes

蔥油餅

Green onion pancakes are popular in China. I like to fry these pancakes in a cast iron skillet to get a lovely golden crispiness. As green onion pancakes are served throughout China, there are regional differences, from thin and flat to thick ones. There are even some leavened with yeast, but this recipe relies on steam for a slight puff, and the oiling of the dough, before the rolling process, to produce flaky layers. Enjoy these pancakes, and do not worry—you will not turn into a donkey by eating them.

INGREDIENTS

2	cups	all purpose flour
¾	cup	hot water

FILLING

2	tbsp	vegetable oil
2	tsp	pure sesame oil
½	tsp	salt
½	tsp	white pepper
2-3		green onions, chopped

EQUIPMENT

- measuring cups & spoons
- liquid measuring cup
- cutting board
- chef's knife
- medium bowl
- fork

- 3 small bowls
- pastry brush
- rolling pin
- cast iron or heavy skillet
- spatula or egg lifter
- kitchen shears

METHOD

1. Put flour in medium bowl and make a well in the center. Pour in the hot water all at once. Mix with a fork (more hot water may be needed) until a soft dough is formed. Place the dough on lightly floured surface and knead into a smooth ball. Place the bowl upside down over the ball of dough and let rest for 20–30 minutes.

2. In a small bowl, combine 1 tbsp vegetable oil and the sesame oil. In another, combine the salt and white pepper.

3. After resting the dough, roll it into a log and divide into 4 equal pieces. Working with one piece at a time (keeping remaining pieces of dough under the bowl to prevent dough from drying out), roll dough into a thin rectangle.

4. Using a pastry brush, brush the oil mixture onto the dough's surface, leaving a strip along one long side with no oil. Sprinkle ¼ of the salt-pepper mixture evenly over the oiled surface followed by ¼ of the chopped green onions. Tightly roll the dough toward the edge with no oil. Pinch to seal the edge of the roll. Then roll to form a uniform cylinder while gently stretching the log to make it slightly longer. Coil the log like a cinnamon bun, and pinch the end of the coil in place. Using a rolling pin, flatten the coil until it is a ¼-inch-thick pancake. Repeat for remaining pieces of dough and filling.

5. Using the cast iron frying pan or skillet, heat 1 tbsp vegetable oil over medium-high heat until hot enough to bubble around the end of a chopstick or wooden spoon. Add one pancake and fry on medium heat until golden (about 3 minutes). Flip the pancake and cook the other side until nicely golden and dough is translucent. Repeat until all the pancakes are cooked.

6. Use kitchen shears or chef's knife to cut each pancake into quarters. Serve warm. If you wish, serve with a dipping sauce made with equal parts soy sauce and rice vinegar.

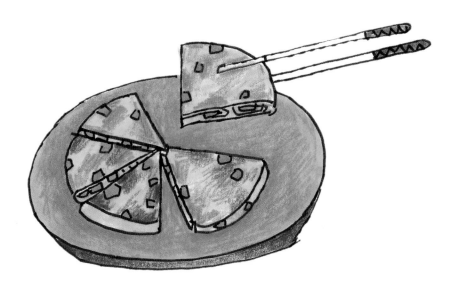

The Hall of Contented Cravings

全滿意樓

Long ago, there lived a king who loved to eat. Each evening he sat down to a lavish feast of tender meats, crisp greens and savory soups. But every now and then he dressed as a commoner, sneaked out of the palace and wandered through the countryside. He visited tea stalls, markets and inns, looking for new and delicious dishes.

In the seaside city of Da Hai, the king saw a long line of people standing outside a restaurant. It was called The Hall of Contented Cravings. He waited in line and finally was seated. He ordered the daily special.

The first plate arrived. He took a tiny bite. His eyes widened. Fine food!

The second plate arrived. He took a bigger bite. His mouth dropped. Very fine food!

The third plate arrived. He ate greedily without stopping. His cheeks bulged like apples. Never before had the king eaten such excellent food.

Back at the palace, the king called for his chief inspector. "I have tasted the best food in the kingdom. Go to the city of Da Hai, to The Hall of Contented Cravings, and bring the chef to my palace."

The chief inspector leapt on his horse and rode to Da Hai. At the restaurant he could not resist tasting the food, and ordered many dishes.

Then he called for the head chef.

A man came out wearing a white apron.

"Are you the head chef?" the inspector asked between mouthfuls.

"No, I am the owner," the man in the white apron answered.

"But I asked for the head chef. His food is so delicious."

"I am also the chef," the man said, wiping his hands on his apron. "My name is Tang."

"I am the king's chief inspector." He pointed to the sign. "What a clever name your restaurant has."

Tang bowed. "We promise that no customer is ever disappointed."

"Come and meet the king," Chief Inspector said. "He wants to discuss food with you."

"Alas, I cannot, I am too busy here."

"You cannot refuse."

"Alas, I'm afraid I must refuse. This is a family business. My relatives depend on it for their livelihood."

"The king will pay you well. You can share your earnings with your family, if you wish."

"Alas, I must humbly refuse," Tang replied, bowing. "I promised my father that I would keep the restaurant open, always."

"I'm afraid the king will be angry."

The chief inspector got up and left the restaurant.

The inspector met the king at the palace gate. "Your Majesty, the meals at that place are marvelous, but the chef will not come."

"Did you speak to the owner?"

"The owner and the chef are one and the same, a man named Tang."

The king frowned. "I will go there myself and speak with him. I am sure he will listen to me."

The next day, the king, surrounded by soldiers and accompanied by the chief inspector, sped to Da Hai.

At The Hall of Contented Cravings, a large crowd gathered. The chief inspector announced, "Make way for the king."

The crowd parted and the king entered the restaurant, followed by the chief inspector.

A salesman and his customer immediately stood up and offered their table to the king, bowing low. A waiter rushed up and took away the half-finished plates, while another waiter scrubbed the table clean. Tang ushered the king and the chief inspector over to their table, bowing deeply. "I shall bring you our best dishes," he said.

"Please do, and after I eat, I want you to come with me to the palace."

"Alas, I cannot leave my restaurant," Tang said, bowing his head. "I promised my father."

"You are a good son," the king said.

"You are truly bold to refuse a king's wishes," said the chief inspector.

But the king said, "Then you must cook some special dishes for me."

"Of course, Your Majesty. I can cook anything you wish."

"So you say. If you don't disappoint me, I will let you stay here. First, cook a dish for me that contains the sky."

People in the restaurant gasped. "Impossible!"

"How can the heavens be put into a dish?"

"Surely that can never be done!"

Soon Tang brought out a bowl of blue and white clear soup.

"What is this?" the chief inspector demanded.

"It's called Sky Blue White Clouds. It contains cloud ears, mushrooms as blue as the sky, and the wings of high-flying birds."

The king took a taste. Delicious! Then he said, "I now command you to cook a dish that contains the sounds of the forest."

The people gasped. "Impossible!"

"How can the sounds of the forest be served in a dish?"

"Surely that can never be done!"

Soon Tang came to the table with a dish of glistening browns, reds and yellows.

"What's this?" the chief inspector demanded.

"It is called Deer in Deep Forest. It contains wood ears, deer meat and wild corn. When you stir the wood ears, you will hear them rustle. When you eat the deer meat, your heart will pound like hooves racing through the woods. When you eat the wild corn, its crunch is like footsteps breaking twigs and branches underfoot."

The king took a taste. Delicious! Then he said, "I command you now to cook a seafood dish. The seafood must be swimming, but it cannot touch any liquid. If you can cook this last dish, I will let you stay here in your restaurant."

The people in the crowd gasped. "Impossible!"

"Surely that can never be done!"

Soon the owner brought out a clear soup of dumplings.

"What is this?" the chief inspector demanded.

"Shrimp wrapped in thin skins of wheat dough. The shrimp floats in soup, but the skin keeps it away from the broth."

The king took a taste. Delicious! "This dish is the very best. You may stay."

Everyone clapped and cheered.

"But I will come to the palace every month on the new moon and cook for you," Tang offered.

To this day, in Chinese eateries around the world, tasty shrimp dumplings are served in soup. They are called won-ton.

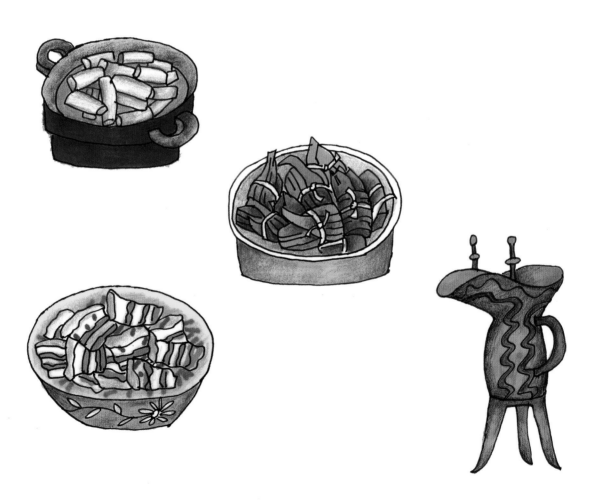

OLD STORY PATTERN

The "impossible task" is found in legends and tales from around the world. These stories feature a villain who has more power than a hero or heroine, and who dictates an impossible task that must be completed. Foolish braggarts and ordinary people fail at the task, but the hero or heroine succeeds by showing great strength, bravery or cunning.

FOOD FIT FOR A KING

The kings of ancient China brought the best foods and the best cooks to their palaces. During China's Zhou dynasty (1045 BC–256 BC), a staff of 2300 people served food to the palaces. They cooked meals for the royal family and prepared food for state banquets and sacrificial feasts. To recognize the importance of food, high-ranking cooks were given official titles and granted nobility.

TWO WAYS TO WRITE WON-TON

In southern China, the Cantonese words for cloud and for swallowing are pronounced wun tun 雲吞 and refer to the wrapped meat dumpling. In northern China, two different Chinese words are used. They are pronounced hun 餛 and tun 飩 and may refer to the muddle-shape of the dumpling. No matter how you write it, won-ton has become one of the best-known soup items on Chinese menus around the world.

Won-Ton Soup

鷄湯雲吞

Won-ton is one of the most popular Chinese restaurant menu items for lunch or as part of a meal. In Cantonese, won-ton literally means swallowing clouds—a good description of its shape floating in delicious broth. The chef at The Hall of Contented Cravings furthered the mysterious allure of these dumplings by solving the challenge given by the king. However, there is no mystery to making these delicious dumplings.

INGREDIENTS

1	lb	ground pork or combination of ground pork & chopped raw shrimp
4		green onions, chopped
1	inch	fresh ginger, minced + 1 slice for broth
½	cup	fresh or canned water chestnuts
2	tsp	cornstarch
2	tsp	soy sauce
½	tsp	salt
¼	tsp	freshly ground pepper
1	tbsp	sesame oil
1	pkg	fresh won-ton skins
1		egg white, beaten
6	cups	chicken broth, homemade or canned low sodium
8	stalks	baby bok-choy or Shanghai bok-choy or Chinese greens
2		green onions, chopped (for garnish)

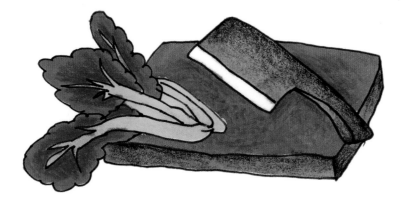

EQUIPMENT

- measuring spoons & cups
- liquid measuring cup
- cutting board
- chef's knife
- medium bowl
- teaspoon & fork
- rimmed baking sheet
- tea towel
- 1 large & 1 medium pot
- colander
- slotted spoon or asian spider ladle
- ladle

METHOD

1. Rinse peeled water chestnuts in cold water and chop into ¼-inch pieces.

2. In the medium bowl, combine the ground pork with the green onions, ginger and water chestnuts. Then add the cornstarch, soy sauce, salt, pepper and sesame oil. Mix together well with clean hands or fork.

3. To wrap won-tons, place 1 tsp pork filling just below the center of a won-ton skin. Then fold the skin in half to form a triangle. Take the tip of the triangle and fold it to touch the longest edge of the folded triangle. Bring the two outside corners together so the tip of the triangle is on the outside, moisten with some egg white, overlap the corners and squeeze to hold in place. Repeat this step with the remaining pork filling and won-ton skins. Keep wrapped won-tons on a rimmed baking sheet and cover with a slightly damp tea towel to prevent them from drying out. They can be refrigerated for a short time or frozen for future use.

4. Meanwhile bring a large pot of water to a full rolling boil to cook the won-tons. Add a pinch of salt. Also bring the chicken stock to a boil in medium pot with a crushed slice of fresh ginger.

5. Prepare the bok-choy or Chinese greens by cutting the bottom of the greens to separate the leaves. Wash in cold water and drain well in a colander. Set aside.

6. In the pot of boiling water, cook won-tons in batches of 15–20. When the won-tons float to the surface of the boiling water, add a cupful of cold water and bring to a full boil again. Use the slotted spoon to remove the cooked won-tons, and place 10–12 won-tons per serving in large individual soup bowls. Repeat this step again to cook enough won-tons for everyone at this meal.

7. While the won-tons are cooking, add the bok-choy or Chinese greens to the boiling chicken stock. Reduce the heat and simmer greens until they are tender-crisp and bright green. Remove the cooked greens with the slotted spoon and divide evenly among the bowls of won-tons.

8. Remove the crushed ginger from the chicken stock. Ladle stock over each bowl of won-tons. Sprinkle chopped green onions on top of each bowl. Serve immediately and satisfy your craving.

West Ocean Greens

西洋菜

Long ago in the south of China, there lived a farmer named Tian. He and his wife grew rice and green vegetables. They had three sons.

As soon as they could walk, the boys helped on the farm. The older they became, the more work they did. If the buffalo fell sick, First Son pulled the plough across the field. If the rains were late, Second Son pedaled the waterwheel and raised water from the river. If weeds invaded the vegetable patches, Third Son spent days pulling them out.

As the sons grew, Tian worried that soon they would marry and start families. Then his farm would be too small to support everyone. There was only enough land to grow rice and vegetables for two extra families, not three.

Which two of my sons should get the land? Tian wondered.

He decided to challenge his sons. He sent them across the ocean to work in the New World. "After two years, come back and bring a gift for me," he said to his sons, as they embarked on a ship. Their mother hugged them and wished them well.

While the sons were away, Tian and his wife worked very hard to grow their food. Each night they were so tired that they fell asleep without even eating. So the neighbors came to help plant and harvest the rice, and their nephews and nieces came to weed the vegetables.

The two years passed quickly, and the three sons finally came home. First Son returned wearing western-style pants held up by metal suspenders. All the villagers gathered at Tian's house to hear First Son's story and see his gift.

"The New World is raw and untamed, so I could not farm. Instead I worked for a merchant. He imported goods from China and Europe. I didn't earn much money, but I had a roof over my head and two meals a day. Here is my gift."

He handed his father a pair of rubber boots. The villagers pushed forward to touch them. They had never before seen waterproof boots. Now Tian walked through the fields and his feet were kept dry.

A week later, Second Son came back. He wore leather boots with stiff soles. The villagers hurried over to hear his story and see his gift.

"The New World is vast, and the towns are far apart. I worked for a firm that hauled goods. Teams of oxen pulled our wagons. We traveled on narrow roads and had to watch for bandits. Here is my gift."

He gave his father a rifle. The villagers pushed forward to touch it. They had never before seen such a weapon. Now Tian could easily scare away the flocks of birds that stole his rice, and could kill the foxes that came to steal his chickens and ducks.

Then Third Son came back. He wore the same clothes he had worn when he left home. The villagers welcomed him and listened to his story.

"The New World is fertile, but the earth is not ready for farming. I worked with a team to clear the land. The first season, the river waters rose and flooded the land. In the second season, we built dikes. Nature is very powerful there. Here is my gift."

It was a small box of earth, with a green plant growing in it. The villagers had never seen such a plant before. They shook their heads, frowned and scoffed.

"What do we need that weed for?"

"It doesn't look tasty."

"Your gift is not worthy," Tian said to his son, casting the plant onto the riverbank. "Your brothers shall get the farm."

Third Son bowed to his parents, hugged his brothers, and set out to make a new life.

One wet day the following spring, Tian pierced his rubber boot by stepping on a sharp rock. His wife tried to repair it with a needle and thread, to no avail.

Soon after that, bandits raided the village, waving knives and axes. They hauled away the rice and vegetables. They stole the seeds. Farmer Tian ran for his gun, but he had no bullets. When he tried to shoot, the bandits laughed and grabbed his rifle.

With no seeds to plant, there was no crop that fall. The villagers went hungry.

One day when Tian was fishing in the river, he noticed a flash of bright green growing on the riverbank. *It's Third Son's gift, the plant he brought for me.* The plant had taken root and had spread everywhere along the embankment— green and succulent. The stems were smooth and sturdy. Tian cut off some of the top leaves and tasted them. They were crisp and sharp to the tongue.

Delicious, he thought. *What a fool I was. Third Son brought me the best gift of all.*

Tian called the villagers to help him harvest the plant. Afterward, they were amazed to see that it grew back so quickly.

That year, the new vegetable fed the village. When the villagers took it to market, they sold it at a very high price, and bought rice, noodles and vegetables. Tian called the new plant *Xi Yang Cai,* West Ocean Green.

"You must find Third Son and tell him how his gift saved the village," said Tian's wife. So he sent First Son and Second Son to find their brother and bring him home.

When they returned, the villagers gave Third Son his own plot of land. "We are so grateful for your gift," they said.

"I regret not seeing what a treasure you brought me," Tian said, hugging his son.

"You are the youngest, but you are the wisest," said his mother.

West Ocean Green became popular in many parts of southern China.

In the West, its name is watercress.

OLD STORY PATTERN

Many European folktales, such as the Brothers Grimm stories The Golden Bird *and* The Golden Goose, *share a similar theme with this story—a king gives a task to his three sons, but the older two fail to complete it. The king doubts his youngest son because of the son's age and lack of experience, but the youngest son insists on trying, and in the end proves to be successful.*

WATERCRESS

Watercress is native to Europe and to Central Asia. With a history of three thousand years, watercress as a food source can be traced back to the ancient Greeks and Romans. One of the first plants cultivated by humans, it only grows in running fresh water. Watercress reached China at the end of the nineteenth century, when it was brought to Hong Kong by travelers.

A CHINESE PROVERB

江山易改,本性難移

Translation: Rivers and mountains easily change;
human traits are hard to move.

Meaning: It's not easy to reform someone.

Watercress Soup

西洋菜湯

I spent many summers working on my uncle's farm where tomatoes, cucumbers and a variety of Chinese melons grew in greenhouses. Between the greenhouses, an abundance of watercress grew in the soggy earth. My grandmother and aunts would make soup from these tender greens. As young children, we nicknamed this soup "ditch water soup." Of course it did not taste anything like ditch water, and we slurped down every last drop.

INGREDIENTS

¼	inch	fresh ginger
1 ½	cups	Poached Chicken (see page 158), sliced, or 8–12 small to medium shrimp
5	cups	chicken stock, freshly made or canned low sodium
1	bunch	fresh watercress, washed, large stems removed
		salt, to taste

EQUIPMENT

- liquid measuring cup
- cutting board & chef's knife
- colander
- teaspoon
- medium pot
- ladle

METHOD

1. Scrape the skin off the ginger piece and slice into thin slivers.

2. Cut poached chicken into ½-inch-thick slices that are bite-sized. If using shrimp, peel, remove veins, gently rinse in cold water and drain.

3. In the pot, bring chicken stock and ginger slivers to a boil. When the stock is at a full boil, add watercress. Once the watercress is wilted and bright green, add chicken slices or shrimp. Simmer, gently heating chicken. If using shrimp, cook until no longer translucent and tinged pink. Do not overcook the chicken or shrimp.

4. Before serving, season with salt to taste.

5. Ladle into soup bowls and serve immediately.

New World Cinderella

新世界灰姑娘

Long ago, when workers from China were helping to build the railways in the New World, a widower named Woo Mah opened a hotel beside the railway line, downriver from town. He had a daughter named San-li.

Soon after he opened the hotel, Woo Mah married a widow. As soon as the widow moved in, she took San-li aside and said, "San-li, the rooms must be cleaned right after the guests leave, and the dishes must be washed right after breakfast, lunch and dinner."

"Yes, Stepmother," San-li said, not wanting to offend her father's new wife.

But soon Stepmother took San-li aside again. "San-li, early in the morning you must feed the hogs and hens, and wash the pig pen and chicken coop, before making breakfast for the guests."

"Yes, Stepmother," San-li said, not wanting to offend her father's new wife.

But soon Stepmother took San-li aside again. "San-li, you must weed the vegetable garden and collect firewood from the forest."

"Yes, Stepmother," San-li said, not wanting to offend her father's new wife.

One day, San-li was so tired from carrying water from the river that she set down her pails and began to cry.

"Don't weep, dear girl."

San-li looked up to see the man who sold fresh fish in the market. He was carrying a bucket of live fish, swimming in water.

"Take a fish home to be your companion," the fishmonger said. "Feed it well, and it will help you."

San-li chose a little fish with silvery skin and bright eyes, and she placed it in one of her pails. As she watched it swim around and around, her own weariness lifted.

Back home she placed it in a fishbowl and fed it tiny scraps of meat, bits of bread and spiders. Everyday she changed the water in the bowl.

One evening, Stepmother called San-li to her room. "The tablecloths look awful," she said. "Wash them tonight, and lay them for breakfast tomorrow. Otherwise I'll tell your father how lazy you are."

San-li took the tablecloths back to her room and sat down on her bed, burying her head in her hands. *How can I wash and dry them by morning? There are so many stains!*

A voice from the fish bowl called out, "Put the tablecloths in a barrel of water. Then drop me in."

San-li went out to the rain barrel, bringing the fishbowl and the tablecloths with her. First she dumped the tablecloths in, and then she dropped the fish into the barrel. The fish swam around and around and up and down through the cloth. The stains vanished like melting snow. Then San-li hung the tablecloths to dry overnight, put the fish back in its bowl and brought it to her room. She fell asleep with a weary sigh.

The next morning before breakfast, San-li laid the clean tablecloths out.

But Stepmother was not satisfied. "San-li, the curtains in the guest rooms are filthy. Wash them now, and re-hang them by nightfall. Otherwise I'll tell your father how lazy you are."

San-li took them to her room and thought, *How can I have these ready in time? There are so many stains!*

A voice from the fish bowl called out, "Put the curtains in the barrel of water. Then drop me in again."

San-li went down to the rain barrel, bringing the fishbowl and the curtains with her. First she dumped the curtains in, and then she dropped the fish into the barrel. The fish swam around and around and up and down through the cloth. The stains dropped off like heavy pebbles. Then San-li hung the curtains to dry in the morning sun, and put the fish back in its bowl.

But Stepmother was hiding behind a tree, and saw how the fish helped San-li with her chores. Her face turned red with anger.

The next day when San-li went to fetch firewood, Stepmother marched up to her room, grabbed the fish and cooked it for her lunch. Then she handed San-li a plate of fish bones, and laughed.

When San-li took the bones to the kitchen, she wept. But soon she heard a familiar voice. "Don't cry, dear girl."

It was the fishmonger, calling through the window. "Hide the bones," he said. "When you need help, toss them into the river and make a wish."

San-li dried her tears, thanked him and hid the bones in her room.

When the lunar New Year arrived, a merchant in town invited everyone to watch fireworks, feast on festival foods and join in a lion dance. He sent his son, Guo, to invite the innkeeper and his family.

When he knocked on the door of the inn, San-li opened it.

"I have come to speak to Woo Mah."

Stepmother came to the door and sent San-li back to the kitchen. As she washed the dishes, she heard Guo inviting the family to town.

"Please come tonight and join the festivities," the merchant's son said.

"We will," said Stepmother.

Later that evening, Woo Mah and Stepmother put on their best clothes and went upriver to join in the festivities, leaving San-li behind to do the chores.

If only I could go, she thought. *Even if I could, I have no fancy clothes to wear.*

Then San-li recalled what the fishmonger had said. She went to the river and placed the dried bones in the water.

"I wish I could celebrate the New Year," she said.

There was a flash of lightning and a roar of thunder, and San-li's dirty apron turned into a jacket of soft silk with vibrant dazzling colors. On her feet were beautiful silk shoes, embroidered with bright flowers. On her wrist appeared a silver watch.

Then the bones changed into a canoe, pulled by giant sturgeons.

"You must leave town before midnight, San-li," the fish called out. "Keep watch of the time. We can only help you until midnight."

San-li stepped into the canoe, and was quickly ferried upriver to the festival.

In town, paper lanterns lit the houses, and the drumbeats of the lion dance echoed through the streets. The sweet aroma of roasting meats filled the air. San-li tasted the delicious foods on display at every stall.

Guo spied San-li in her fine clothes, and he followed her. When she was thirsty, he bought her a nectar of fine fruits. When she was tired, he brought her a sedan chair to rest on.

All night he courted her, but San-li was shy. *He likes me only because of my fine clothes. When I answered the door for him, he didn't so much as glance at me.*

A few minutes before midnight, San-li checked her watch. "I must go," she said to Guo. "You have been very kind to me, but I must rush off."

"Wait! Tell me your name!" he shouted after her. "Where do you live?"

At the river, San-li leapt for the canoe, but just as she was about to step into it, it vanished. San-li landed in the water. Midnight had arrived. She grabbed a log and floated downriver, but all she had left of her evening was one embroidered shoe.

Guo, who had followed her, found the other shoe on the riverbank. *I must find the girl who owns this.*

He asked everyone if they knew the girl with the beautiful embroidered shoes, but no one did.

The merchant's heart ached for his poor son, who had lost the girl of his dreams. "I will give twenty gold dollars if the owner of this shoe comes forward," he promised.

When San-li heard this, she went to town. The merchant frowned at her torn and dirty clothes, and told her to leave his shop. But San-li held up the other embroidered shoe.

"Son, I have found the girl who you met at the festival," the merchant shouted.

Guo ran into the shop, beaming.

"Where are your fine clothes? Where is your silver watch?" he asked, shocked by her appearance.

"I have come for the twenty gold dollars," San-li said, handing him the shoe. "Here is the other shoe. You'll see that it matches." She handed him the shoe.

Guo held it next to the one he had found on the riverbank. "These shoes certainly do match."

San-li took the shoes from the merchant's son and put them on. They fit perfectly. "I have come for the twenty gold dollars," San-li repeated, holding out her hand. "I am going to seek my fortune."

The merchant reached into his pocket and gave her the money. She counted it and walked out of the shop, leaving Guo behind.

OLD STORY PATTERN

Thousands of versions of the Cinderella story have been told around the world. In all these tales, a girl endures a horrid life of suffering, receives magical assistance, finds comfort and lives happily ever after.

In China, a version of this story was written in the ninth century. It features a girl named Ye Xian who lived in a community of cave dwellers. She befriended a fish that was ten feet long.

FISH FOR LUCK AND FOOD

Many Chinese people view fish as a good luck symbol, because the Chinese word for fish sounds the same as the word for abundance. In the past, Chinese children wore good-luck charms in the shape of a fish carved from jade, or cast in metal.

A famous Chinese saying, "Carp hurdles Dragon Gate," tells the story of a fish that swam up the Yellow River against a mighty current. With strength and courage, the carp leapt over the rapids at Dragon Gate. The gods were impressed, so they rewarded the carp by turning it into a dragon. "Carp hurdles Dragon Gate" is a reminder that it takes a lot of effort to overcome hardship. Pacific salmon are also famous for swimming upstream to return to their place of birth.

Steamed Fish with Black Bean Sauce

豆豉蒸鮮魚

My father and uncle loved to go fishing. Much excitement was shown by all when they came home with a fish. Their big catch would be featured as the main course for dinner that evening. My mother would maintain the fresh fish flavor by steaming the fish with ginger and green onion or with a black bean sauce. At the end of the meal, all that would remain were the fish bones. Although these fish bones did not have magical powers to grant a wish, as in the story, our fish dinner created great family memories.

INGREDIENTS

1	lb	white fish fillets such as cod, red snapper, halibut
2-3		green onions
2	tsp	fresh ginger, julienned
1	tbsp	black bean sauce
2	tsp	light soy sauce
2	tbsp	canola or corn oil
2	tbsp	cilantro, chopped (for garnish)

EQUIPMENT

- measuring spoons
- liquid measuring cup
- cutting board
- chef's knife
- paper towels
- shallow heatproof dish or glass pie plate
- plastic wrap
- wok or wide, deep skillet with lid
- steaming rack
- oven mitts & tongs
- fork
- small pot

METHOD

1. Check fish fillets for any bones, and remove. Pat with paper towels to remove any excess moisture.

2. Place fillets in a single layer in the shallow heatproof dish or glass pie plate. Cover with plastic wrap and refrigerate until ready to steam.

3. Wash green onions and shake off excess water. Cut off root ends and discard. Cut the green onions diagonally into thin slices and set aside.

4. Place the steaming rack in the wok or skillet. Add water so that it does not touch the bottom of the rack. Bring to a boil.

5. While the water is coming to a boil, evenly spread the black bean sauce over the fish fillets. Sprinkle half of the ginger over the fish.

6. Using the oven mitt and tongs, carefully place the dish of fish on the rack above the boiling water. Cover the wok and steam for 10–15 minutes over reduced heat but enough to maintain steam. If the fish fillets are thick, then the cooking time will be longer. The fish is cooked when the flesh is easily flaked with a fork. While the fish is steaming, be sure to check the water level to maintain the production of steam and to prevent the wok from being boiled dry.

7. Carefully remove the heatproof dish from the wok using oven mitts and tongs. Pour off any liquid from the plate into a glass liquid measuring cup and set aside.

8. Sprinkle the thinly sliced green onions and remaining ginger over the cooked fish fillets. Drizzle the light soy sauce over the fish fillets.

9. Heat up the canola or corn oil in the small pot until it is hot but not smoking. Carefully pour the hot oil over the fish. This will result in a crackling sound as the hot oil hits the fish, and it may splatter.

10. Heat the reserved liquid, and pour over the fish.

11. Garnish with cilantro if desired.

12. Enjoy with steamed rice and stir-fried vegetables. Make sure that you savor all the flavor by spooning some of the liquid mixture over your rice.

NOTE: This recipe uses prepared black bean sauce or black bean with garlic sauce that can be found in the Asian food section of local supermarkets. This recipe also works without black bean sauce.

The Ungrateful Wolf

中山狼傳

One day long ago, Old Scholar was traveling along a forest trail leading a sturdy mule.

Suddenly a big grey wolf came limping up, panting from exhaustion and hanging his head. "Kind sir," said Wolf, "please help me. A hunter has been chasing me all day and night."

Old Scholar was kindly, and hated to see any living creature harmed. He took an empty sack and gestured for Wolf to creep in. Then he tied it up and strapped it on the mule's back.

Soon, a hunter galloped up on his horse, carrying a bow and arrow and a heavy sword. "Old man," he asked, "have you seen a wolf running through the forest?"

Old Scholar shook his head. "No, I haven't." *That's the truth,* he thought. *The wolf was limping, not running.*

"Well, watch out for a hungry wolf," the hunter said before galloping away. Soon the forest was quiet again.

"Kind sir," Wolf called from inside the sack. "Please let me out now."

Old Scholar opened the sack and let Wolf out. Once free, Wolf shook himself fiercely, bared his huge teeth and lunged at Old Scholar, who darted to the other side of the mule.

Then Wolf crept behind the mule, but it kicked out, hitting Wolf on his head.

Wolf howled.

"I saved your life," shouted Old Scholar. "How could you try to eat me?"

"I love the taste of meat," Wolf said, lunging at him.

Old Scholar swiftly climbed up a nearby tree. "Have you no conscience?"

"The law of nature is this: the strong crush the weak," replied Wolf, circling. "Nature has no conscience."

"But don't you decide what you must do and what you must not do?"

Wolf paused and sat down on his haunches.

"Wolf, I'll come down off this branch, and together we'll walk along the path. Whoever we meet, we will ask which of us is right—you or I. If three agree with you, then I will let you eat me. If three agree with me, then I will go free."

The hackles on the back of Wolf's neck softened. "Agreed."

Old Scholar picked up the sack, placed it on the back of the mule, and they walked on until they saw an ancient apricot tree.

"Let's ask that tree," Wolf said.

Old Scholar bowed to the tree. "Wolf says there is only the law of nature, and nature has no conscience. Does Wolf owe me mercy because I helped him?"

The leaves of the tree rustled in the wind. "My apricots provided food for the farmer and his family for forty years. Now that I am old and produce less fruit, he told his son to chop me down and sell my wood. Wolf does not owe you anything. There is only the law of nature, and nature has no conscience."

The delighted wolf smiled. "I love meat," he growled. "One down, and two to go."

Old Scholar, Wolf and the mule walked on until they saw an ox tied to a fence.

"Let's ask that old ox," Wolf said.

Old Scholar bowed to the ox and explained the problem. "Wolf says there is only the law of nature, and that nature has no conscience. Does Wolf owe me mercy because I helped him?"

Ox tipped his horns up and his nostrils flared. "I ploughed the rice fields for the farmer and his family for twenty years. I pulled his cart to town and back. Now that I am old and stiff, the farmer plans to slaughter me. He and his family will feast on my meat, tan my hide into leather, and use my horns to carry water. Wolf does not owe you anything. There is only the law of nature, and nature has no conscience."

The delighted wolf jumped up and down. "I love meat. Two down, and one to go."

Old Scholar, Wolf and the mule walked on until they met a farmer loading bags of rice onto a wagon.

Old Scholar bowed to him and explained the problem. "Wolf says there is only the law of nature, and that nature has no conscience. Does Wolf owe me mercy because I helped him?"

"Wolves break into my garden and eat my chickens. When the snow falls, and the sheep get lost in the hills, wolves attack them and feast on their flesh. How did you allow yourself to get mixed up with a wolf?"

"I saved Wolf from the hunter."

"A person should never help a hungry wolf." The farmer turned to Wolf and asked, "How did Old Scholar save you from the hunter?"

"He hid me in a sack," answered Wolf.

Farmer took the sack off the back of the mule and held it up. "Do you mean this small sack?"

"Yes. That's the one."

Farmer looked skeptical. "How could a giant wolf like you fit into such a tiny sack?"

"I pulled in my legs and rolled into a ball."

Farmer laid the sack flat on the ground. "I don't believe you," he said, frowning. "Show me how."

Wolf pawed the ground and crept inside.

Then Farmer slipped his belt off, tied the sack up tight and threw the bundle onto his wagon.

"You were right, Wolf," Scholar called, as Farmer drove away. "The strong crush the weak."

OLD STORY PATTERN

In stories such as Little Red Riding Hood, The Three Little Pigs *and* The Boy Who Cried Wolf, *the wolf is seen as something evil. This view came from farmers and shepherds who worked hard to protect their farm animals against predators.*

Other legends saw the wolf in a more helpful light. Many stories tell of wolves providing milk to human infants. These tales include Romulus and Remus *and* The Jungle Book.

Talking animals have long been featured in folktales. Storytellers combined animal and human traits into a single character in order to tell a better story. For example, the cleverness of wolves helped to make a villain seem scarier, or the nervousness of chickens helped portray mindless panic—as in Chicken Little.

SCHOLARS VERSUS FARMERS

In The Ungrateful Wolf, *the author pokes fun at a respected figure in Chinese folklore, the scholar, who is frozen by fear and inaction. The farmer, less respected than the scholar, turns out to be the clever one who saves the day.*

A CHINESE PROVERB

騎牛找馬

Translation: Ride cow to look for horse.

Meaning: Take on something second-rate while seeking something better.

Beef Lettuce Wraps

生菜牛肉包

This traditional Cantonese dish is popular at banquets that feature Chinese delicacies. At Chinese Lunar New Year, lettuce leaves are hung at the front door because lettuce is symbolic of new life or growth. This dish can be made with squab, chicken, duck, pork as well as beef. It is eaten like a burrito with the filling rolled inside the lettuce leaf. Like the wolf hiding in the sack, the delicious meat filling is hidden in a lettuce leaf just waiting to be eaten.

INGREDIENTS

1	lb	medium or lean ground beef
1	tbsp	soy sauce
1	tbsp	cornstarch
½	tsp	sugar
1		medium cooking onion, chopped
1	inch	fresh ginger, minced
2		garlic cloves, minced
2–3		green onions, chopped
8	oz	canned water chestnuts, drained and chopped
8–12		iceberg or butter lettuce leaves, cleaned and dried

SAUCE

1	tbsp	soy sauce
¼	cup	hoisin sauce
2	tsp	sesame oil

EQUIPMENT

- measuring cups & spoons
- cutting board
- chef's knife
- medium bowl
- can opener
- teaspoon

- colander or salad spinner
- large skillet
- spatula
- slotted spoon

METHOD

1. In the medium bowl, combine the ground beef with soy sauce, cornstarch and sugar. Set aside.

2. Chill lettuce leaves in the refrigerator, taking care to keep them whole so they can be wrapped around the beef filling.

3. In the skillet over medium-high heat, brown and crumble the ground beef mixture. When beef is no longer pink, remove from skillet with a slotted spoon to drain excess fat.

4. Leaving about 1 tbsp of fat in the skillet, sauté cooking onions until translucent. Add the ginger, garlic and green onions, and stir-fry to bring out aroma, then add the water chestnuts. Return cooked ground beef to skillet. Then add the soy and hoisin sauces and the sesame oil. Stir to combine and cook for about 2 minutes or until hot. Remove from heat.

5. To serve, spoon warm beef filling onto each lettuce leaf, and wrap like a burrito. Eat and enjoy.

Two Gods: One Wise, One Not

山上二神

Once upon a time in China, there was an ancient village in a fertile valley between two high mountains. The farmers and families who lived there thought that the good soil and good weather were gifts from two gods—one who lived in a temple on North Mountain, and one who lived in a temple on South Mountain.

Years passed. The sun grew hotter and less rain fell. Harvests shrank, so the farmers and their families had less food to offer the gods.

One day, a boy in the village fell ill with a fever. Cups of herbal teas and rolls of cold wet cloths couldn't cure him. So his mother climbed South Mountain and prayed in the temple. Her prayers were not answered.

The next day, the mother climbed North Mountain and prayed in the temple.

That night, North Wind whispered:

> *To heal the child, come back and climb.*
> *Watch your step and take your time.*
> *At the temple is a tree.*
> *Cut the bark to boil some tea.*

The mother hurried up the mountain again and collected bark from the tree in front of the temple. She took it home, boiled it up and fed it to her son. Soon he was running around in perfect health. To thank the god of North Mountain, the boy's family took three steamed chickens, three barbecued ducks and a roast pig to the temple. It had been a long time since so much tasty food lay on the altar.

The god of North Mountain invited the god of South Mountain to dine with him. They crunched through crispy skins and chewed on juicy meats. They licked their fingers and toasted each other.

"I was so hungry," said the god of South Mountain. "I haven't had a decent meal in months. How did you get all this tasty food?"

"A boy in town was sick, and I told his mother how to heal him."

One day in the village, a rice farmer's daughter fell sick and wouldn't wake up. No amount of shouting or shaking could get her to open her eyes. Her father climbed South Mountain and prayed for help at the temple.

This is my chance, thought the god of South Mountain. *If I help the villagers, I will get lots of food.*

That night, by his daughter's bed, the father heard South Wind whisper:

To heal the child, come back and climb.
Watch your step and take your time.
At the temple is a tree.
Cut the bark to boil some tea.

The god of South Mountain's mouth watered at the thought of eating plump juicy chickens.

Meanwhile, the father hurried up South Mountain. But there was no tree growing at the temple there—not in the courtyard, not anywhere near.

How strange, he thought. *The wind said to come here.*

So he went inside and knelt before the statue of the god. "Oh mighty god, please tell me what to do. Only you can save my little girl."

Then he smelled cedar. He looked up. *Why, the statue is carved from cedar wood. The god of South Mountain must mean for me to cut a piece off the statue.* So the farmer took out his knife and cut a small piece of wood from the back of the statue.

At home, he boiled it up and fed it to his daughter. Soon she was running around in perfect health.

To thank the god, the girl's family took rice and beans up South Mountain and set them at the altar. They brought no meat because they raised no animals and only grew crops. They also swept and mopped the temple's floors, and re-papered the windows with rice paper. It had been a long time since the temple looked so clean.

But the god of South Mountain was angry because he hadn't received any steamed chickens, any barbecued ducks or even a roast pig. To make things worse, he now suffered terrible pain whenever he sat down.

So he went over to the god of North Mountain to complain. "You got steamed chickens, barbecued ducks and roast pig. All I got was rice and beans."

"Rice and beans make a healthy meal too," his friend said. "Was it in your heart to help that man?"

The god of South Mountain hung his head in shame.

"Next time, use sincere words of your own."

"You're right. I was just thinking about the tasty food."

The god of North Mountain laughed and laughed, and the god of South Mountain joined in. When he laughed, he couldn't feel the pain.

And he didn't even feel hungry.

STORY SETTING

This story gives us an idea of the setting from which many folktales come. Before the modern era, before big cities and electricity, most people in Europe and Asia lived and worked on farms, growing their own food. They were at the mercy of nature. Farmers and their families suffered if there was too much or too little rain. Often there wasn't enough food to feed everyone.

They were also at the mercy of disease, as they were unsure of the cause of illnesses and how to heal sick people. Children were especially at risk. So people turned to various gods and spirits for help. They believed that if they showed respect to the gods and spirits, then they would reap a good harvest and receive protection from disease.

CHINESE GODS

In the Chinese tradition, some human beings were turned into gods because of their great deeds, such as bravery in battle or showing great love for their parents. In this way, some gods were very much like humans—imperfect.

CHINESE TEA

The tea in this story is herbal medicine tea. For centuries, Chinese doctors relied on natural products to help control pain, heal illnesses and treat injuries. Medicinal tea is made using minerals, plants such as roots, leaves, mushrooms, tree bark and flowers, or animal parts such as horns, fur and marine creatures.

A CHINESE PROVERB

遠 山 望 著 那 山 高

Translation: *Looking from this mountain, that mountain looks tall.*

Meaning: *The grass is greener on the other side.*

Poached Chicken
with Green Onion and Ginger Sauce

姜葱白切鷄

Poached whole chickens are a popular offering at shrines, when asking for blessings or thanking the gods. After the blessing, my family takes the chicken home to serve at dinner that same evening. My mother would make this dish frequently and then use the light chicken stock for cooking or for making soups. This dish is my favorite comfort food, and I am glad that I do not have to compete with the god of South Mountain for this delicious tender chicken.

INGREDIENTS

3	lb	whole chicken, chicken breasts or legs
1–2		fresh ginger slices

GINGER & GREEN ONION SAUCE

¼	cup	canola or corn oil
2	inches	fresh ginger, minced
4–6		green onions, minced
2	tsp	salt

EQUIPMENT

- measuring spoons
- liquid measure cup
- cutting board
- chef's knife
- fork

- large pot with lid
- tongs
- colander
- small pot

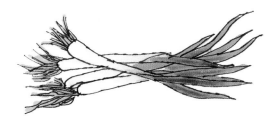

METHOD

1. Bring large pot of water to a rolling boil, leaving enough space for chicken.

2. On the cutting board, smash the ginger slices with the blade of the chef's knife to release some of its juices. Add the smashed ginger to the boiling water.

3. Submerge the chicken in the pot. You may need to hold the whole chicken down with tongs until the cavity fills with water to weigh it down. Bring the water back to a full boil. Then cover with a lid and reduce the heat to medium. Simmer the chicken for 15 minutes.

4. Remove from heat, leaving the lid on the pot. Let the chicken cool in the pot (about 1 ½–2 hours). Test the chicken for readiness by piercing its thickest part with a fork or paring knife to see if the juices run clear and the chicken is no longer pink.

5. Remove the chicken from cooking liquid with tongs, allowing excess liquid to drain. Rinse the chicken under cold water.

6. Cut chicken into inch-thick slices. Arrange on a serving platter.

7. In a small pot, heat up canola or corn oil until hot but not smoking. Add the sauce ingredients to the hot oil. Serve this sauce on top of the chicken slices or on the side as a dipping sauce.

NOTE: The cooking liquid can be used for making sauces, or reduced to ⅔ of its original volume by simmering, uncovered, to make stock for recipes such as the won-ton soup or the congee. This stock can be frozen for use later.

Notes on Sources

The stories *Stretch and Fold, Stretch and Fold, Hall of Contented Cravings* and *West Ocean Greens* are original works written by the author based on folktale and fairytale motifs.

A Wondrous Pear Tree is from the famed collection of tales *Liao Zhai Zhi Yi* 聊齋誌異 written in 1679 by Pu Song Ling 蒲松齡. An early English translation is *Strange Tales From a Chinese Studio*, by Herbert Allen Giles (London, 1880).

Banquet of Waste was broadly adapted from *The Punishment of K'uang Tzu Lien* in *The Eight Immortals of Taoism: Legends and Fables of Popular Taoism* by Kwok Man Ho and Joanne O'Brien (New York, 1990).

The Schoolmaster's Autumn Festival was broadly adapted from the Shaoxing opera *Xia Xiu Cai Guo Nian, Scholar Xia Celebrates the New Year*. It appears as *Mr. Yeh's New Year* in *The Ch'i-lin Purse: a collection of ancient Chinese stories*, retold by Linda Fang (New York, 1997). The date of the original story is unknown, but Fang set it in the Ming dynasty because it was a historical period in which many Chinese opera stories were set.

Monkey Fights White Bone was broadly adapted from the Chinese classic *Journey to the West, Xi You Ji* 西遊記 by Wu Cheng'en 吳承恩 in the sixteenth century.

Steamed Bread and Salt was broadly adapted from *The Story of Salt* 鹽的故事 by Xiao Zhongyou 蕭中游 in *The Lady in the Mirror* 鏡中人 from *Zhong guo gu dai mian jian gu shi cong shu* 中國古代民間故事叢書 (Hong Kong, 1967).

Third Lady of Plank Bridge is from *Huan Yi Zhi: Strange and Unusual Records* 幻異志 by Sun Wei 孫頠. His work is from the Tang dynasty (AD 618–907). The story appears in English in *Chinese Prose Literature of the T'ang period AD 618–906* by Evangeline Dora Edwards (London, 1974).

New World Cinderella is a variant of a story that has hundreds of versions from around the world. The Cinderella story known in the West was first recorded in French in 1697 by Charles Perrault. An earlier version of such a story about a girl named Ye Xian 葉限, set in third-century China, was recorded by Duan Cheng-shi 段成式 in a collection called *You Yang Za Zu* 酉陽雜俎. That story was retold by Ai-ling Louie in *Yeh-Shen: a Cinderella story from China* (New York, 1982).

Some scholars trace *The Ungrateful Wolf* back to the Tang dynasty (AD 618–907) and Song dynasty (AD 960–1279), where a story called *The Zhongshan Wolf* 中山狼傳 was attributed to several writers. The story was also developed into a four-act *zaju* 雜劇 play as well as a single-act *yuanben* 院本 play.

Two Gods: One Wise, One Not was broadly adapted from *The Two Earth Deities* in Wolfram Eberhard's *Folktales of China* (Chicago, 1965). Used with permission.

Magic Rice on the Mountain was adapted from *The Sacred Rice in Fairy Tales of China* (Cassell, Plc, London, England, 1959, later a division of Orion Publishing) written by Peter Lum, non-de-plume of Lady Bettina Crowe (1911-1983). The author's attempts to trace the copyright holder were unsuccessful.